THE
SKATEBOARD
DETECTIVES

D1079278

In memory of Miloš Vainer and with great thanks

THE SKATEBOARD DETECTIVES

Diamonds are for Evil

ANDREW FUSEK PETERS

ORCHARD BOOKS

ORCHARD BOOKS
338 Euston Road, London NW1 3BH
Orchard Books Australia
Level 17/207 Kent Street, Sydney, 2000, NSW, Australia

First published in 2008 by Orchard Books
A paperback original

ISBN: 978 1 84616 608 2

A CIP catalogue record for this book is available from the British Library.

1 3 5 7 9 10 8 6 4 2

Typeset by SX Composing DTP, Rayleigh, Essex
Printed in Great Britain by CPI Cox & Wyman, Reading, RG1 8EX

Orchard Books is a division of Hachette Children's Books, an Hachette Livre UK company.

www.hachettelivre.co.uk

1. FLIGHT

Saturday 29 September, 2.45 am – the present

Break shuffled up to the ledge of the flat roof, pulled back his hood and peered over. The face that checked out the very long way down was framed by a mop of black hair. The skin was pale and hinted at too much food with a high grease content. Brown eyes nervously scanned the scene, looking for trouble.

Four storeys below, the shop fronts were shuttered and bolted. By day, this pedestrianised alley thronged with the rich and wannabe wealthy, looking to make the deal of a lifetime. Now there was only a staggering drunk, busy recycling his dinner onto the pavement. The man stumbled off and the gang were ready to go.

'No way,' Break hissed. Heights were not his thing.

Ben's rangy form was curled up in the corner, trying not to shiver. 'What do you mean?' he whispered back. 'You've done it before.'

'Falling into a river is one thing, but ending up as the filling in a concrete sandwich is another.' Break put his skateboard down and started scratching the scabs on his elbow. He'd popped some decent air in his time, but this was suicidal. His last jump had been a smooth nollie off a set of twelve steps. The move was good, and he had even managed to land at the bottom with a textbook tail manual. That's when it all went wrong: hitting the ground with two wheels followed by a perfect bloody elbow slide. Bad bailout. He had no desire to repeat the experience.

'Stop squabbling, you two,' said Charlie, with an exasperated look on her face. 'The point is, how do we get over?'

The sheer drop was bad enough and the vicious wind, whipping up the chip papers and ruffling their hair, didn't help matters. The gang looked across at their target – a flat roof on the other side of the alley, about ten metres below, the edge helpfully surrounded by razor wire. The gap between the buildings would have tested the best long jumpers, but this was the point where the alley was narrowest.

'I say we forget about the whole thing! What we're doing isn't exactly legal. Most other teenagers would be tucked up with a decent computer game by now,' San muttered miserably, hugging his rucksack.

Ben stood up and pushed back his short dreadlocks. 'Don't be a wimp, Gadget Boy. It doesn't suit you. It looks like I'm the only one who's man enough to do the job!' He walked backwards across the roof, counting his steps. 'If I can get enough of a run up...' He bent down at the back edge and sprang forwards. One, two, three, four – by the fifth step he'd reached the edge and come to a perfect full stop, as he contemplated the drop below and the huge jump he might be mad enough to take on.

'Good. Let's do it. Charlie, have you got the rope?'

Charlie resented being dogsbody, but Ben was taking the risk. Fair enough. 'Here. Top Gun 8.1 mm. Should have no problem carrying us lot.' She began to unloop the coil to give Ben plenty of slack. The oversized satellite dish in the corner would provide anchor. She quickly attached one end of the rope with a tautline hitch. 'Good luck!' she whispered as she handed the other end to Ben.

Ben was nervous as he began warming up. He stretched his hamstrings, made a few squats and circled his arms. 'The art of a good traceur is fluidity!' he said. 'Watch and learn. A saut de détente followed by a roulade should do it.'

'I'm sorry,' interrupted Break, pointing at his watch. 'Did we ask for a free-running lecture? Could the great Ben himself be scared?'

Ben frowned. Break was right. He was terrified. Once again he stepped back. Rehearsal time was over. He crouched down, feeling his heart beating double-time and the blood pumping in his veins. This was it. He wrapped the rope round his forearm and sprang forwards. Total focus now. Four steps, but the fifth was the one that counted. His knee bent and he ricocheted into space.

If the street drunk had bothered to look up, he would have seen a boy in flight and wondered if the booze was making him hallucinate.

For Ben, time crawled by. He could feel the dirty air of the city make a slipstream round his body. The street below was picked out in perfect detail, every streetlamp and jeweller's shop front, even the endless chewing gum acne suffered by pavements the world over. This was the moment he lived for and the reason why birds were on to a good thing. Just for a split-second, he'd beaten gravity.

The trajectory was good. It had better be, or the slam would be terminal. No more Ben. If only his mother could see him now. Or maybe not.

He tucked his knees in as the roof rushed up to meet him. Every millisecond counted. If the landing was even slightly out, he'd have the joy of seeing his leg bones shooting out of his kneecaps. It didn't bear thinking about. A gap-jump was one thing, but the landing and the roulade – or roll – was another.

BANG! His feet skimmed past the top of the razor wire and thumped onto the roof. Years of practice in his mum's gym and on the streets paid off as he tucked his head in, leaned diagonally and curled into a ball. The single motion cushioned the impact as he rolled perfectly across the leaded surface to finish by standing, the end of the rope still in his hand. Yes! Yes! Yes!

He quickly turned and gave the thumbs-up to the others and a quick bow. This would out-YouTube all those other posers by a mile. Wild applause was the right response, but given the circumstances, not a good idea.

Now he had to make the rope fast enough to support body weight. A bulky lightning rod would have to do. He attached the cable tension adjuster and began to ratchet in the slack. Soon, the rope was taut. He ran to the edge of the roof and looked into the street below. All clear.

Meanwhile, San was busy unpacking his rucksack and took out three metal loops. 'Clip-on loop-ends. This is loopy – how can such a tiny bit of metal carry me?' San wasn't exactly fat, but he was certainly bigger than the skinny girl in front of him.

Charlie smiled. 'San. Give me credit. I've been doing this stuff since I was four.'

'Yeah, but a circus-skills workshop in a warehouse with safety netting doesn't count!'

By now, Charlie had attached each of the loops to the rope and rigged up the harnesses, helping Ben and San to climb in. 'Who wants to go for a ride?'

San scuttled slowly over to the edge. His eyes went wide. The alleyway looked like a Lego model, with bins so tiny he could have picked them up and stuck them in his pocket. He felt dizzy. 'Ladies first!'

'Oh, San, it's the twenty-first century, you

know. After you! I insist!'

Before San could object, Charlie pushed him out into the void. The rope bowed and San shut his eyes, trying not to scream as he slid into space. It was like aeroplanes. Despite all the science, there was no way those big lumps of steel had any business being in the sky. Neither did he. His stomach gave a lurch. If he looked down, he'd be showering the pavement with every item of food he'd eaten in the last twenty-four hours.

The next thing he knew, Ben had caught hold of him and stripped off the harness.

'See. Easy-peasy, mate.'

'It's alright for you.' San trembled all over, wishing he were back in his nice, safe bed. But at least he was still alive.

Charlie was next. She leapt off the parapet as if jumping from high-rise buildings was an after-school hobby. The loop slid smoothly towards the middle of the street and she readied her legs for landing.

She heard a sudden slicing sound above her head and looked up with horror as the outer plastic sheath of the rope began to shear, cutting a wedge into the nylon core. Both the rope and the gang's well-honed plan began to unravel.

Charlie's harness ground to a halt halfway between the building and a good twenty metres above the ground. She hung there, swaying like a Christmas decoration.

If the rope split, she'd plummet onto the road below. Pizza topping for tarmac. She gulped as two faces looked up at her from the roof, so tantalisingly near. What could she do? There was only one thing for it. She lifted a leg out of the harness and manoeuvred herself backwards until she could get her foot onto the padded bum strap. Holding onto the rope above her, she slowly stood up, swinging back and forth in the breeze.

Charlie froze as someone shouted, their voice echoing along the lonely lane. She looked down and breathed a sigh of relief. It was only the drunk, singing to himself. He stumbled along the pavement, peering into each doorway and dragging a shopping trolley behind him, filled with all his worldly belongings. She watched, fascinated.

Once the man had decided on his spot, he parked the trolley and pulled out a bed roll. Perfect. A room with a view and added air-conditioning.

But then the man did something very stupid. He staggered and found himself falling against a plate-glass window. There was a moment of silence as the security system had a quick, logical think, and then decided it was time to make a lot of noise.

The alarm wailed out, alerting the world that all was not well. The drunk acted as if the electronic screeching was no more than a soothing lullaby. He slowly slid to the floor. But the sleeping tramp was the least of Charlie's problems. Within what seemed like a few seconds, she heard sirens approaching fast.

Ben shouted at her, but she couldn't focus as she desperately tried to hold onto the rope above her head. Her normally agile hands refused to do as they were told. Safety was so near and yet too far. Come on Charlie! She started to kick the harness away. But it was too late.

The sirens grew to a crescendo. A police car came screeching round the corner and pulled up almost directly beneath her. Two officers got out and began to scan the scene. If they looked up, she was so dead.

2. ROPE TRICKS

Saturday 29 September, 3.10 am – twenty–five minutes later

Charlie could recognise that self-important swagger anywhere. PC Smythe had once told her she would follow in her father's footsteps. If the officer turned his head too far upwards, his nasty prediction would come true. It wouldn't be easy to explain why a freckled twelve-year-old with a boyish haircut was hanging from a rope in the middle of the night. The only advantage her bird's-eye view gave her was a glimpse of the officer's badly hidden bald patch and his dandruff-decorated shoulders. Fat lot of good that would do her.

The rope creaked. This was it, then. But for some strange reason, the police declined to look up. Their eyes had spotted the cause of all the disturbance.

'Alright, Alf?' The shapeless form slumped in the doorway was not-so-gently prodded with a polished black toe-cap.

'Ummmff!' grunted Alf, none too pleased to be woken from his dream of a bed in a four-star hotel after a sumptuous meal of steak and hand-cut chips. He opened his eyes. Reality was always such a let down.

'There are good places to kip and, Alfie boy, this isn't one of them. Come on!' PC Smythe hauled the man to his feet as the other officer rang the security company. False alarm. As if by magic, the wailing stopped, to be replaced with loud complaints as Alf was pushed down the alley and told to find himself alternative accommodation. As he shuffled away, he offered up several interesting hand-signals along with a vocabulary that made Charlie smile.

'What a waste of time!' said PC Smythe.

His colleague nodded, wiping his hands on his trousers as if trying to get rid of Alf's all-too-overwhelming body odour. 'We should be catching real criminals.'

If only they'd known how close they were. They got into the car and slowly drove off.

Break leant over and looked down.

'You alright?'

'Just!'

Charlie wanted to leap down into the road, run after Alf and give him a great big kiss. But her problems weren't over yet. She was still stuck twenty metres above the alley on a rope that was fraying too quickly for comfort. Freeing the harness was not an option, as the loop was embedded deep under the plastic. She'd have to hand-walk it.

Charlie checked her grip. Good. It was time to move. She finally kicked her legs free of the harness and let her hands take the weight. Gloves would have been helpful as the rope felt far too slippery.

First, she had to deal with the harness itself. There was only one way it could be done. Charlie swallowed and tightened the grip in her stronger, left hand. With her right, she let go of the rope. That four fingers and one thumb were her only protection from sudden vertical descent didn't bear thinking about. Her free hand fumbled with the clip – which, with its easy single-handed operation, was supposedly designed for climbers. Well, the adverts were wrong, as the supposedly state-of-the-art catch remained stubbornly closed. She had no choice. If the harness came off and fell into the street, it would give the game away. Finally, the clip came undone and she tucked the useless straps into the back of her jeans.

Now all she had to do was reach the other side of the alley. Her arms were already killing her and the hard work had only just begun.

The trick was to think like a monkey. She'd done it thousands of times before. Ben's mum, Mrs Olatunji, was always talking about shifting your weight. It was like a pendulum. One hand in front of the other, testing the grip each time. Ben and San egged her on as she inched agonisingly nearer the lower roof. The angle of the rope was steep and it was all she could do to stop her hands sliding. Her fingers felt sweaty and the hard tarmac below was bad news all round.

As she approached the roof, the rope began to stretch. There was nothing Ben could do. If he ratcheted it up again, the whole thing might snap. Sure, eBay was good most of the time, but second-hand rope? What had she been thinking? No point worrying now. She was almost close enough to touch the roof, but the rope had slipped below the edge and into the razor wire.

Ben and San tried to lift it, but with her weight

pulling it down, they had no leverage.

She was stuck. Again. She felt tears pricking her eyes and her muscles were screaming. Maybe she should let go? Chance the drop? She knew the statistics on people falling from heights were not on her side. She'd heard somewhere that babies bounced due to their soft bones. But though the others called her a baby sometimes, twelve was a little bit too old to rely on that theory.

She thought about the parallel bars at Mrs O's gym. Ben's mother was a fantastic teacher and Charlie's dismounts had won awards. This was no different, except for the lack of a welcoming rubber mat on landing. There was no time to think about it. She began to swing, using her body to build up momentum.

'What are you doing, girl? Are you crazy? The rope's gonna snap!' hissed Ben, but she ignored him.

Back and forth. Back and forth, higher and higher. The core of the rope was beginning to unravel, the strands separating out. She'd only have one go at this, so it had to work. As she swung forwards and reached the highest point, she let go, feet first, her body acting as a rocket with the rope as its launch-pad. Charlie continued the move she'd made countless times, arcing up and over, then curling into a backward somersault. In midair, she gave a sideways twist, aiming her body at the roof.

She felt the razor wire slide past, within a centimetre of her face. Some poor pigeon hadn't been so lucky and its mangled feathers almost tickled her cheek. Her training paid off. Miraculously, instead of freefalling to a sticky end, or being sliced up by thin slivers of metal, she landed feet first, stumbling forwards into Ben's arms. It wasn't ten out of ten, but it would do. She felt out of breath, exhausted, the adrenalin still rushing through her system.

'That, girl, was amazing!' Ben held Charlie's shaking shoulders to calm her down.

'Your move wasn't too bad, either!' she said, trying to ignore the burning pain in her fingers.

There was a groaning sound. The rope had had enough. The tension Charlie had exerted finished the job and it snapped like a bullwhip. It was the last thing they needed.

As they stared helplessly, it swung across the street, harmlessly slapping against a wall that had no alarms buried in the bricks. The loop clattered off, to join the other bits of rubbish littering the pavement. This time, no police cars came rushing up the alley. There was nothing to see, no crime in progress. The city could sleep on in peace. Ben pulled the remains up the wall to hide the evidence.

Then he felt his phone vibrate. It was the signal from Break on lookout. All clear. Charlie was sitting down, getting her strength back. San was checking his rucksack to see if all his kit had survived. From the dim light that filtered up from the street, Ben could see the sweat on his mate's skin. The next bit would be up to him and panicking was a strict no-no.

'Now, all we have to do is break in, foil the security, blow a safe and steal a diamond.'

3. LEARN THE DRILL

Saturday 29 September, 3.30 am – twenty minutes later

The flat portion of the roof was a rectangle about ten metres by five. At the back, a more traditional structure sloped up at an angle, covered in overlapping tiles.

Sanjay put down his rucksack and pulled out a stethoscope.

'And what is your diagnosis, Doctor Musa?' Ben paced up and down. Slow stuff annoyed him.

'Hole-itis, hopefully!' San moved the end of the scope over the whole lower part of the roof, tapping each tile and listening carefully. 'The secretary mentioned a leak, remember? I put two and two together and worked out that this building has a weak point... Got it!' The echo in his ears was decidedly hollow. 'This is where we'll make the first incision!' San used a pair of pliers to bend back one of the lead tile fixings as Charlie pointed a pencil torch at it. Twelve tiles later, they had uncovered a sizable oblong of roofing felt.

'Scalpel!' said San.

Charlie passed over the Stanley knife and watched as San sliced through the roof's protective membrane. Within a minute, the oblong had become a dark hole.

Even Ben was impressed as he peered in. 'That's good. How'd you do it?'

'Simple. All I had to do was rely on the great British builder and his reputation for laziness. Why board out a loft that no one lives in? It's so dark that their employers would never notice, except when the rain comes in. Their short cut is now ours.'

Ben wasn't so sure. 'What about the alarms?'

'Not up here. Look at this roof,' said San, pointing out the coils of razor wire to stop intruders climbing up the outside. 'It's like Fort Knox already. Theoretically, no human could ever make it up here. My friends, we are... unexpected!' He pulled three sets of potholing headgear out of his rucksack and passed them round. 'Wait til we're inside before turning on your headlights.' He also handed Ben and Charlie a pair of rubber gloves each.

San stepped into the hole and switched his lamp on, revealing an attic space filled with cobwebs, dust and empty cardboard boxes. The others clambered in behind him. 'Give me five mins.' One by one, he slid the tiles back into place and then reattached the cut-out felt with black gaffer tape. He pulled out a can and began to spray. Instant cobwebs. Who needed hi-tech when your local joke shop would supply?

San put his fingers to his lips. He had no idea if there were sound sensors. They moved carefully forwards, placing their feet down gently, testing for creaking floorboards. Their headlights turned the attic into a cave. They could almost have been explorers in uncharted territory.

At the edge of the space, a dark stairwell led downwards. San pulled out a can of glitter hairspray.

Ben couldn't hold back. 'Now is not the time to be worrying about your appearance!' he whispered. 'Does this look like a fashion show?'

San gave him his best withering stare and sprayed the space ahead of them. The glitter hung in the air, lit up by the torchlight. As the spray began to fall, it revealed the stairwell's perfect security system. Every other step had a low-level red laser beam shooting across it. Walk through the beam and all hell would break loose. His note-taking had paid off.

'A little hop, skip and jump, Ben. Right up your street!' whispered San. 'Off you go!'

Ben took the stairs two at a time, stopped at the bottom and looked up. Charlie came next. Before San started down, he pulled out his phone, slid it open and punched the buttons for the web browser function. He carefully tucked the phone in his shirt pocket and contemplated the glittering beams. Six steps later, he was down. Compared to the rope slide, this was child's play.

Ahead of them lay the cutting and polishing room. The workbench, with its spinning disk and ancient circular saws, lay silent. A single, red light winked at them from the corner of the room.

Ben froze. 'I don't want to make you nervous, but surely that light can see every movement we make.'

'Chill out, Ben!' San pulled his phone from his pocket. 'Found this out on the net. My browser's signal acts as a negative field, informing our friendly motion detector that no one is in the house. I'm amazed the manufacturers haven't cottoned on. It only works with some makes, so our last visit paid off.'

They walked unhindered through the dark room and into the office. San leant over a desk and turned on a small anglepoise lamp. The tinted windows on both sides of the room meant that seeing out was fine, but privacy was guaranteed, which suited their purpose perfectly. 'Headlights off. We're here.' He pointed the lamp at the alcove in the far wall, where a huge lump of metal squatted. 'The Chubb Sovereign, grade 8. Weight: 3,400 kilos.'

'We won't be taking that home in our backpacks!' said Charlie. No one smiled.

San pulled what looked like an overgrown machine gun out of his bag. 'Your dad told me about the old safes, Charlie. One whack with a sledgehammer at the right spot and you'd shatter the hinges. The makers got wise, and this door has mild steel on both sides with a nice sandwich of extra-hard concrete. Bash it as much as you like and all you get is a few dents and an aching arm. As for oxyacetyline or thermal lances, forget it – unless we want to set the whole place on fire.'

San plugged the tool in and on the end of it fixed what looked like a plastic loo-roll with serrated edges. 'But this, my friends, is the business. Diamond-core drill. Amazing what a bit of compressed carbon is capable of. Our diamond-embedded cutting edge will go through anything – aluminium, aloxite. You name it.'

'How d'you get hold of kit like that?' asked Ben.

'*Gizmoid* magazine must be desperate!' answered San. 'My dad normally tests underwater laptops, PDAs that also do your toast, and other useless stuff for those who have it all but know that gadget nirvana is just round the corner. Then, they sent him a bunch of drills. Great cover copy – "Who's the hardest of them all?" And this baby was the winner! As they say – set a crow to catch a crow!'

'Are you trying to be clever?' said Ben.

'No. I *am* clever. There's a difference.' San carried on his lecture. 'Our only drawback is the noise. But did this stop the great Sanjay Musa? No. Our school Design and Technology department was the perfect place to experiment. I told the teacher I had an idea for helping builders keep their hearing!' San pulled out what looked like two halves of a giant tea-cosy, stuffed with moulded foam, and fitted them round the drill. 'Guns have silencers. Why not a drill? This is only the start. With the patent, I'll make millions.'

He turned to Charlie and asked her to point him in the right direction.

San positioned the drill midway between the two locks on the safe door and pressed the trigger. A smile split his face as the only sound to escape was a small hum. Ten minutes later, he felt the metal give. There was a faint smacking noise as he switched the drill off and pulled it from the door.

The light showed a perfect hole about three centimetres across, cut right through the door. Small wisps of smoke still curled off the metal edges. The smacking noise had been from the cut-out cross-section falling through the other side.

'Hmm!' said Ben. 'You're in danger of giving a good name to nerds.'

'Thank you! Thank you!' San turned to Charlie. 'All done. Your turn now.'

Charlie had grown up listening to stories of her dad's escapades. Instead of Snow White and Rumpelstiltskin, the fairy tales she'd been told were filled with bolt stumps, lever packs and multiple relockers...until he got caught. But that was another story.

She looked at Ben and San. 'We don't even need to open the door.'

'What?' said San. 'After all this, you can't pick it?'

'You're not listening. I didn't say *can't*. Have you got the fibre-optic scope?'

San pulled out what looked like a long bendy snake made of metal links with an eyepiece on the end. 'I don't get it.'

'No, but I will.' She bent down and pushed the snake through the hole, sliding a button at the side to light the other end. After a few moments of wiggling about, a small sigh escaped her lips. 'Ah!'

'You two are driving me nuts!' said Ben through clenched teeth.

Charlie pulled the scope out and took a stick of lip salve from her pocket. She explained as she took off the lid and twisted the bottom. 'They told us last time how diamonds stick to anything greasy.' Charlie smeared the salve liberally on the underside of the scope. 'I'm simply taking the principle and reapplying it.'

She bent to the hole again and inserted the scope while the others waited impatiently.

Charlie hoped her eyes weren't deceiving her. There! She pulled back the scope and lowered it by a fraction of a centimetre. Now she had to keep her hands from trembling as she began to withdraw the scope. One wrong movement, and she'd lose it.

'Have you...?'

'Shut up, Ben!' she said through pursed lips as she pulled the scope out of the hole. Her fingers wavered and there was a slight scraping sound. As the end came out, she twisted it round to reveal the greasy underside. It was empty.

'That's impossible!' Charlie wanted to scream. It was too late. Thanks to her stupid shaking, it would have dropped down the inside, well beyond the reach of any scope, and time was running out and she had let them all down...

'Charlie!' said San gently. 'Look!'

She turned round. 'Oh, wow!'

'Now that is class!' said Ben.

Resting right on the edge of the drilled hole, winking at them like a stoplight, lay a stone. A very special stone that flared out with an intense light-purple colour. The Botswana Pink.

'Bit girly, that colour!' said Ben.

'Yes, and that's because diamonds are...'

'A girl's best friend. Yeah, yeah.'

Charlie stepped back. 'Go on, Ben. You got us here. But don't drop it this time!'

Ben knelt down as if in prayer and scooped the diamond into his palm. To think that some people would pay so much money for such a tiny object. It was incredible.

'Right, Ben. When you've finished falling in love, we have to leave.' San sat down in a swivel chair and began sliding his hands under the desk in front of it.

Ben stuck the diamond in the safest place he could think of – his mouth. It nestled under his tongue like a tooth that any tooth fairy would die for.

'Please don't swallow!' said Charlie. 'I, for one, wouldn't want the job of digging for it as it comes out the other end.'

'Thanks for spelling it out!' grimaced Ben. 'By the way, your taste in lip salve is disgusting. Cherry Burst? Eurgh!' They both looked at the steel-lined door that was the only exit.

'Don't worry!' said San. 'These places are built to keep people out, not in. And every one of them has emergency release systems. Even better, they override the alarms. Otherwise, every employee going outside to have a quick fag would summon half the city's police force. All I did was observe the secretary and put two and two together. Here we go!' San had found the button. The door silently slid open.

The other two made for the exit. But San had one last job to do. No break-ins had made Tirov & Sons lazy. The video feed should have been connected into a remote location. But the wiring led to one place only: an unassuming cupboard high up on the office wall. It wasn't even locked. Within seconds, the DVD of their exploits was stashed safely in his pocket. This was never going to be an internet favourite. The others beckoned to him. He closed the cupboard door and allowed himself a small smile of satisfaction.

The building let go of its intruders without even a whimper. They stood waiting in the doorway as San sent a short text to Break. The answering vibration told them the street was free of the one thing they really didn't need – people.

One by one they ran down the lane, round a corner and into an alleyway stuffed with overflowing bins. Ben held his nose as he opened the nearest one. 'Not the best-smelling stash point in the world!' he whispered as he handed the other two their boards.

Then they were off, cruising the back byways of the city, their wheels clicking out the rhythm of freedom and success. Charlie 50-50ed the kerbs and Ben spun some perfect vaeriel tail-flips, jumping every bollard as if challenging the city to an obstacle fight. San pushed and puffed along behind, merely trying to keep up. They were welcome to their tricks, he thought.

As they carved round a corner, Ben felt the weight fall off his shoulders. They'd done it.

'Evening, kids!'

A figure stepped out of the darkness. What he held in his hand was enough to persuade them all to skid to a halt. This was a different type of silencer. And on the end of it was a gun.

4. THE BOWL AND THE BULLY

Saturday 15 September, 3.45 pm – two weeks earlier

Break stood at the edge of the bowl, surveying the scene. The park had only opened two weeks ago and the place was packed. For once, the council had got it right. He'd heard a rumour that the adults had even consulted skaters over the construction. It was a grey world out there but sometimes miracles happened. He wanted to bend down and kiss the concrete, but thought better of it.

The park was a thin triangle of old wasteland sandwiched between two busy roads. It was divided into a flat area, with ramps and humps for street skating, and the bowl. The engineering was outrageous. There was a small mini-vert, like a stretched half-pipe. This blended seamlessly into a huge hole dug into the city, carpeted in the smoothest, most velvety concrete he'd ever known. This was one seriously sexy gap in the ground.

BMXers were lined up on one side, skaters on the other, everyone desperate to drop in first.

An older woman stood by the edge of the bowl, wearing shades and a thick coat, even though the city was having its own miniature global-warming induced heatwave. Probably some mother, checking that her child didn't die of injuries received. It took all sorts, he supposed. He looked around, sensing the microsecond of opportunity. A biker gave him the nod as he balanced his tail on the edge of the ramp.

'Are you ready, San?' he shouted.

San stood on the other side, DVD cam at the ready. 'Do it!' he replied as the red light on the camera began to wink.

Dropping in was always a rush, like riding a rollercoaster without any safety harnesses. There was no holding back. His front foot pushed down on the board and he teetered over the edge, letting gravity do the work. Before he could even think, he was up the other side, grinding the rail backside with both trucks in a sliding 50-50. Then he swooped down again and headed into the depths of the bowl. The sheer walls loomed up above him. What was he doing, beetling down like some insignificant insect into the mouth of a towering tsunami? It was a monster ride. He crouched down to hit the far corner and pump it for speed.

He remembered his dad, holding him by the arms and whirling him round and round when he was tiny. He had always shouted, 'Faster! Faster!' And his dad would oblige until they both collapsed on the ground in a dizzy heap. This was better. He whirled round the pool, crouching up and down, building up velocity until he could feel the wheels complaining. Like a slingshot, the board shot out towards the far edge.

It was now or never. That was the thing with all the moves. You had to commit. He didn't bother with an indy-grab, but let the board take him up the vertical wall as he kicked back the tail and flew out into the sky. The next thing Break knew, he was taking off straight over the bodies of the astonished spectators. They craned their necks to catch his motion. Who needed a jet-pack? Ricta cores and decent bearings were the only machinery he needed to soar through the grimy city air.

Break wasn't done yet. Flying was one thing.

Landing was another. He could see the concrete rushing up to meet him. He bent low, praying to the god of polyurethane. The prayer worked as his wheels hit the ramp with his body where it was supposed to be. He swooped up the other side and ollied out over the edge as every single skater began to smack their boards on the edge of the pool, louder and louder until the noise was deafening. The bikers tried to look bored, but Ben clapped him on the shoulder.

'That was one radical stunt!'

San came running as Break bent over, trying to catch his breath.

'Did you get it?' he panted. The thought of having to make history twice over was not appealing.

'Yeah. Every second! By this time tomorrow, when I've uploaded the footage, you'll be top hitter on every video server, I promise.'

Break glowed all over. It didn't get better than this.

There was a strange lull, like the moment at a party when everyone stops talking. Suddenly, the pool was empty as the skaters wandered off to grab drinks loaded with as many E-numbers as possible, stuff down sarnies and gossip about who pulled off what and where.

San seized his chance. He handed the camera to Ben and scrambled down into the small half-pipe. He put down his board and pushed off. As he rode up, he bent his knees like he'd been told until the board came to a full stop. Then gravity took him backwards. This was the moment he normally fell, but Break had lectured him about going with the flow, letting the board take you. And now it did. He was fakeying! Back and forth, higher and higher as he built up speed. No one took any notice, but as far as he was concerned, even though his board was wobbling all over the place, this was way up there with the first man to walk on the moon. Even Break gave him the thumbs up.

'It's Gadget Boy with his little toy!' snarled a voice in Break's ear.

Four wheels good. Two wheels bad. 'Alright, Baz? Didn't know you could rhyme, and putting that many words in a row must have been tough for you. Well done,' said Break to the boy who had ridden right up to the gang on his bike.

Baz didn't like that. 'What you talking about?' He sat back on the saddle as he tried to work out the insult. The boy was the same age as them, but bigger in all areas, including muscles, thanks to the long hours of biking and lifting papers during his evening round. He sported the latest haircut – nothing, apart from a close-shaven fuzz. He looked like a genetically modified blond polar bear.

'Never mind,' said Break, turning away.

Behind Baz was an assortment of other bikers, all in the same year at school. It was a tribal thing. There were Goths and nerds, bikers, bladers and skaters. Most BMXers were OK. They kept to the etiquette of the parks, taking it in turns for the rides. But Baz's lot didn't bother with the rules.

'When you get bored with that cheap little pop tart of yours, we might let you have a go at some real grown-up stuff.' Baz pulled out a handkerchief and polished the spindles on his wheels.

'Thanks mate, but toddler bikes don't really do it for me. Have you taken off your stabilisers yet?' Break wasn't going to let his good mood be destroyed by this jerk.

'Toddler bike?' Baz's blotchy face went even redder. 'Sunn hubs and rims, three hundred quid. DK six-pack frame, four hundred. I could go on.'

'Oh, please don't. It only proves that you know how to spend your dad's money. As for talent?'

'Why don't we see, eh?' Baz turned to look at the pool, noticed San still pootling away at the bottom of the ramp and gave what he thought was his most vicious smile.

In a game of chicken, Baz lifted the handlebars and rolled into the pool, straight towards San.

'Out of my way, Car-Crash Kid!' he shouted. There was a horrified silence, as if his words went far further than any punch ever could.

They all knew the story, but friends also knew it was a no-go area.

San had been two years old and strapped into his car seat. His mother never saw the monster van pull out of nowhere and shunt the car off the road, crumpling it like paper. He was untouched. His mum was dead. The van vanished into history, leaving only a cruel nickname.

'Oi!' shouted Break. But it was too late.

San saw the huge bike thundering towards him and lost his nerve. The board slid away from his feet. Break had learned how to fall. It was an art. Always better to roll than crash. But San was in a different league. His body crunched into the concrete as the other skaters booed. San rolled over, trying to wipe his face so no one would see the tears as pain shot through his left hip.

Break leaped in, retrieved the board and pulled San to safety. San limped to the side, feeling humiliated and beaten.

Baz ignored both of them as he whipped round the bowl. On the first vert, he reared up the side and let the bike take him out. Midair, he made the 180 turn and slipped back in. This time, as he hit the other side, his whole body slipped off the bike, until only his hands held onto the handlebars. The skaters deliberately turned away as the bikers chanted, 'Superman! Superman! Superman!'

He went one step further. As he hit the air and let his body fly free of the bike, his left hand snaked down to grab the saddle. For a split-second both bike and body resembled some impossible hovering sculpture.

'Superman seat grab!' sighed one of his cronies, as Baz finished off the manoeuvre and leaped out of the bowl to thumb his nose at Break.

'You were saying something about talent, *Arthur*?' he sneered. The boys around him creased up with laughter.

Break bridled. No one called him by his real name and got away with it. He raised his board, but Ben pulled him back.

'He's not worth it. Why pay so much attention to a lump of bacteria?'

Baz was on a roll now. 'Oh, and so sorry about your dork of a friend. Poor thing, involved in yet another crash. Tell him to leave this place to those with real skill, eh?'

San gave him a stare like sharp blades. If only looks really could kill. It wasn't as if he could even remember what his mother looked like these days. Only a bunch of photos on the mantelpiece and the sense of something big missing in his life. No wonder his dad worked all hours. He'd have that Baz one day. Not yet, but soon, when he was ready.

Break pushed Ben's arm away and stepped closer. 'You're all mouth, Baz. Funny how you like to pick on kids weaker than you. Isn't that what cowards do? How about you and me, right now, right here?'

Baz's smile fell from his face. He was bigger, but there was a wild look in Break's eyes that made him uncomfortable. 'I'm not scared of you.'

Break stood his ground. 'That's settled then. Come on.' Break put down his board and walked forwards, keeping his eyes fixed on Baz's face, daring him to look away. San and Ben could only look on helplessly. You never knew with Break.

'Whoa!' said Baz, trying to hide his nervousness. 'I was only having a laugh.'

'Maybe you should say sorry to my friend.' Break's voice was almost a whisper as he motioned to San.

Baz had had enough. He slid the bike round and hared off, his cronies peeling away to follow. 'We'll be seeing you,' he shouted back, before vanishing round the corner.

Break wanted to chase after him, smash the arrogant, spoilt brat's nose. 'Yes, we'll be seeing you for sure!' he muttered to himself, then turned to the gang. 'Are you alright, San?'

'I'll live,' his friend grimaced. The fall was nothing. It was the words that really hurt.

'Good, time for you to hit the bowl. It's like falling from a horse. You gotta get straight back on again.'

'Hmm!' said San. 'Tell me again why it's uncool to wear pads?'

'Scars, bruises and near-death experiences. It's what the streets are all about!' intoned Break.

'You really talk a load of rubbish sometimes. Cheers for sticking up for me, though!' And as San limped back into the bowl and did his best, even the die-hard skaters who'd learned the basics back in infant school slapped their boards as applause for his efforts.

5. AN UNEXPECTED VISIT

Sunday 16 September, 11.30 am – the next morning

They could smell the perfume even before they opened the door. Break's nose wrinkled as a woman with dyed black hair and enough make-up to sink a ship came wafting in.

'My darling Benjamin! How you've grown!'

Break mouthed the word *Benjamin* at San as they both tried not to laugh. Charlie stared at them with disapproval.

'Aunty Reliza?' began Ben. 'It's been a...'

But before he could continue, the woman was off. 'Long time. And look at you!' She bent over and pinched his cheeks. 'No one's called me Aunty in years. Still, your mother and I did grow up together! And these must be the twins? Their names?'

'Mary and Grace. Three years and counting,' said Ben, his normal confidence squashed under the overwhelming presence of the woman who handed her fur-trimmed coat to Charlie as if she were a cloakroom attendant.

'I hope you're not too old for chocolates. Handmade by my old friend Louis Grinoille in Piccadilly. Organic, of course.' She delved into her hand-stitched leather bag and pulled out a pink box tied with a bow.

'Thanks!' said Ben. No, he was never too old. A sweet tooth was for life, not just for childhood. When he'd been younger, she'd always turned up bearing gifts, and Ben was only too happy to be the recipient. The twins looked on greedily with puppy-dog eyes. 'Alright then, girls...' He turned to Ms Reliza. 'Do you mind if I open them?'

'Naturally. That's what they're for!' Her smile revealed a perfect set of white teeth.

As the chocolates were handed out and introductions made, Ms Reliza sat down on the sofa, wriggling around uncomfortably. She finally pulled out a piece of Playmobil from under a cushion and set it down disdainfully on the carpet. 'I heard about your poor grandma and popped into the hospital to see her. She looked very run-down, poor thing.'

'Yeah. Baba's not been well for a while. But they reckon, with the antibiotics kicking in, she'll be right as rain in a few weeks. Mum and Dad are out at work, baby Thomas is at nursery and I'm on duty today.' Ben grimaced as one of the twins spat out her chocolate straight onto the carpeted floor, deciding that additive-free confectionery did not do it for her.

San stood up. 'I'll get a cloth.' He limped off to the kitchen, his hip still hurting from the day before.

'I thought I'd pop by and see how you were doing, and...' Ms Reliza leant forwards. 'I wanted to talk to you. In fact, all of you. Is it possible you could find something to amuse the little ones?'

Ben was puzzled but tried to be polite. 'Well. Sure. I'll set them up with a DVD. Mary? Grace? Fancy watching *Spot the Dog*?'

The girls needed no persuasion and were soon happily glued to the screen.

'We can talk in the kitchen, I guess.' Ben led them all through the door. There was a small table that the rest of the gang managed to squeeze round. The woman stared at the remaining stool as if it were an affront to her posterior, but finally gave in and sat down.

'Last week, I met a very interesting man at the launch of his new exhibition of Fabergé eggs. Mr Yevtushenko?' She looked at the children, watching their reactions. Now she had their attention.

Only a few weeks ago, San, Break, Charlie and Ben had foiled a plan by one of the top city gangs to steal the almost priceless Lilies of the Valley egg. Their reward from Mr Yevtushenko, the rightful owner, was currently sitting in the bank, earning some healthy interest.

'Until you came along, he'd decided the education system in this country was failing badly. He has since revised his opinion. I was so proud to hear that the son of my old friend had played a part.'

Ben couldn't help smiling. 'You're very kind, Ms Reliza.'

The woman waved away the compliment. 'I told him that I had a serious problem and his suggestion was that I get in touch. So here I am.'

Charlie broke in. 'We got lucky. That was all. A bunch of kids in the right place at the right time.'

'That's not what I heard, sweetie. Breaking and entering, taking on criminals, out-chasing cars – the list is endless. You do yourselves a disservice! The point is, someone has done *me* a disservice.

They've stolen what is rightfully mine and I want you to steal it back for me!'

The gang sat back, gobsmacked. Break spoke for them all: 'Lady, we don't steal.' He folded his arms and stared at her.

'At least listen to what I have to say, before you make up your minds.' Suddenly, Ms Reliza lost her look of glamour. Her eyes seemed uncertain and all the make-up in the world couldn't cover the fact that she was upset.

'Your mother and I were close at school, even though I was as interested in gymnastics as she was in the endless rocks I dug up on weekend trips into the country with my dad. Geology fired me up, but one stone got to me in particular – crystallized carbon. It starts life two hundred kilometres below the earth's surface and gradually moves up over millions of years through volcanic pipes. These pipes are made of a material called kimberlite. But it's what lies inside the pipes that became my great obsession.'

Break stared out of the window. Lectures were not his thing at all. The sun had come out and he was desperate to skate. San interrupted his daydreams.

'You're talking about diamonds!' he said.

Four sets of ears perked up.

'Yevtushenko was right about you lot,' smiled Ms Reliza. 'When I read about them at school, the whole world of diamonds seemed like a fairy tale.' Her eyes stared off into the distance. 'Little did I know that, twenty years later, it would be my living.'

Break cut in. 'Thanks for your life story, Ms Reliza, but what's this got to do with us?'

'Sorry. I was rambling. My speciality is the fancy-coloured stones. It's a niche market, but some shades increase the value per carat hugely. Canary yellow is good, blue is interesting, but fancy pink is the rarest.'

'What? Like bubblegum?' said Ben.

'A little bit more valuable than that!' Ms Reliza looked at each of them. 'I'd heard about a stone that no one wanted to go near. It was a 15-carat beauty. The only problem was its clarity.'

As she carried on, Break's thoughts about hitting the vert went out of the window. He, and all the others, were hooked.

Ms. Reliza continued. 'Every stone is classed on a scale from "Internally Flawless" to "13", meaning imperfect and with inclusions visible to the naked eye.'

'And the flawless ones are where the big money is,' said San.

'Precisely. Maybe I should take you on as an apprentice!'

San preened himself until Ben tried to give him a dead leg under the table.

'So there was a stone for sale, reputed to have been given by an Arab prince to his mistress. But nobody wanted to buy it, since, under magnification, you could see an inclusion that all the experts agreed was caused by a tiny particle of iron oxide. Even worse – it was this fault, they said, that gave the stone its colour. Before I bought it, I'd heard that all the famous cutters – Asher, Missaef and Horowitz – wouldn't touch it with a bargepole.'

'So why did you buy it?' asked Break.

'Hear me out. Life is about risk. You all know that – it's what makes people winners or losers. I had a feeling about this rock, a gut instinct perhaps, that this baby was make or break. I sold everything I had and bought it...at $60,000 a carat.'

'But that's...' Charlie tried to do the sums in her head.

'Just under a million dollars, sweetie. My life savings. Was I mad?'

Nobody dared nod their head.

'I bought it secretly. If it went wrong in the

cutting, I would be the laughing stock of the trade. I went to the best cutters, Tirov & Sons. They had one of the last British polishers in their workshop – most of the trade now goes to India and China. But the man on the wheel had a reputation: Tom Jenkins. His dad was Sam Jenkins. Of course, you wouldn't know but the family go way back. He looked at my stone under the loupe and said to me, *I'll do it, Ms Reliza, but if it goes wrong, you can take the fall.*

'The saw was up and running. I couldn't bear to look, so I left him to it. A day later, we had lost a carat, and still the inclusion was there. He asked if I wanted to continue. I had no choice. The rest of my life was riding on the result. Each week, I came by and the stone was smaller and each carat lost was $60,000 down the drain. Then I got the phone call.'

Ben couldn't help it. 'And...?'

'And...it was like winning the Grand National. The inclusion had gone. And the Gemological Institute of America was happy to certify that my 15-carat imperfect stone had become a flawless, intense pink, marquise cut, 10.01-carat diamond. When Maximilian Tirov invited me into the workshop, I couldn't hold back the tears of joy. He opened a bottle of pink champagne and we dropped the stone in a glass full of the liquid – you couldn't even see it!

'I gave old Tom a big kiss – his face went red – but he was proud of his work. There was a tiny bit more polishing to do, so it was agreed I would come round the next day to pick it up – and that's when everything went horribly wrong.' Her face clouded. 'I gave them that stone under a gentleman's agreement. There were no receipts and nothing in writing. But so much for trust! The next day, I went back to find that old Tom was off sick. Mr Tirov invited me into his office and asked me what I wanted. I thought he was joking at first. I told him I'd come for my diamond and he just looked at me, and said, "What diamond?"'

'That's outrageous!' said Charlie.

'Thank you. I know.' Ms Reliza pulled out a handkerchief to wipe the tears running down her cheeks. 'None of the staff would meet my eye and I realised I had been duped. They had the stone and I had no way of proving I owned it.'

'But couldn't you go to the police?' asked Ben. 'You know, show them your receipt for buying the stone in the first place?'

Ms Reliza fiddled with the clasp of her handbag before answering. 'I, er, I haven't been totally straight with you. Some of us still do business in the old way – I have a life-long aversion to paying tax to the Inland Revenue so I do most of my business in cash.'

'That's a bit dodgy, isn't it?' interrupted Break.

'I suppose you're right. But I'd taken the risk. I didn't want to hand over half the reward to the government! Maximilian Tirov knew how I'd acquired the stone. That was his trump card. If I went to the police, I'd be investigated and all sorts of things might come out.'

'So now, you want us, a bunch of secondary-school students, to get your diamond back?' asked Break, incredulous.

'Absolutely.' The thought seemed to cheer her up. 'And when I sell it, for ten times what I paid for it, five per cent will go to you.'

Charlie did the sums. The reward from Yevtushenko was good, but this was unbelievable.

'I'm sorry,' said Break, 'but why not hire the professionals?'

'A bit of tax avoidance doesn't make me a criminal!' she snapped. 'So how would I find them? And you're my last chance. Otherwise, I lose the house, my car, everything I've worked for. And Tirov & Sons run a careers education day for secondary school pupils. It would be the perfect opportunity to find out where the diamond is and make your plans. Mr Yevtushenko stressed that your skills were...extraordinary.'

'Well, when you put it like that...' Ben was clearly excited.

Break stood up. 'Listen, Ms Reliza. We appreciate the offer, but – hang on a second. I remember now. You were at the bowl yesterday!'

The others looked puzzled, but Ms Reliza merely smiled.

'Dark glasses and an overcoat even though it was hot.' Break's memory was pin-sharp.

'Well spotted! Like you, I do my research. I was impressed by what I saw.'

'That's true. I can make a few moves!' admitted Break, allowing a smile to cross his normally serious face. 'It's hard being top of the game!'

Charlie butted in. 'What Break means, when he's finished his bout of self-congratulation, is that we'll think about it.'

Ms Reliza stood up. She shook their hands formally but left Ben to last, kissing him on both cheeks and leaving behind a pair of very expensive lipstick tattoos and an embarrassed teenager. She pulled out an embossed business card and handed it to him. 'Here's my mobile number. Ring me any time, day or night. They're bound to try to sell the diamond on quickly, so if you can help, we must move fast.' She looked at Charlie. 'My coat, dear?'

Charlie bristled, but found herself doing as she was told and going out to fetch Ms Reliza's coat.

'Benjamin, do send my love to your parents! And don't tell them about this – I'm sure they were worried enough about you last time.'

Ben nodded. She had a point. The last thing he wanted was his mum and dad involved. He could see it now – his dad pacing up and down the worn-out living room carpet:

'No way, Ben. Are you mad? Mum and I can only pay the bills with me doing endless hours in your uncle Don's taxi company in the evenings. What are you thinking? And if you get caught breaking into a diamond dealer's, whose story will the police believe?' He'd have a look on his face that said his son was yet one more worry to add to the pile.

But that was it. Ben wasn't mad. What if *he* could do something about those mounting bills? It might involve breaking the law. But hey, life was too short.

'...And please, please help me with this terrible injustice!' Ms Reliza implored before sweeping out of the house, leaving the gang somewhere between excited and gobsmacked.

6. HOMEWORK

Tuesday 18 September, lunchtime

'It's mad!' said San. 'I mean, look at us!' They all sat on the edge of the playing fields, ties undone, panting in the late summer heat. 'We don't exactly resemble hardened criminals!'

'Speak for yourself!' said Ben, bouncing about on his heels and trying out his best Mafia strut.

Break nodded his head. 'This isn't our problem. I feel sorry for the old lady, but...'

'She's not that old!' broke in Ben.

'Oooh!' said Charlie. 'I think the dreadlocked boy is in lurve!'

There followed a variety of lip-smacking and slurping noises, which Ben bravely ignored.

'Hey. She's my mum's oldest friend and it sounds like she's in trouble.'

'So?' said Break.

'There's more to it.' Ben stopped pacing and faced the group. 'My mum told me that there was this boy at school who was giving her a lot of grief – ripping up her homework, following her to school, nicking her lunch money. Mum was in pieces.' Ben looked off into the distance. 'Thing is, her mate stepped up. Mum never knew what she did. One second, the guy was in her face. The next, he's got his arm in a sling, broken in three places, and he's acting the mouse. Ms Reliza told my mum she'd never have to worry about him again.'

'Impressive!' said Break, grudgingly.

'So now, her old school friend is calling in the debt…' said Charlie.

'Something like that. I'll give Ms Reliza credit, though, she never mentioned it again.'

The others finally fell silent.

'We're starting to sound like the three musketeers!' said Break. 'You know, all for one and one for all!'

'Except,' said Charlie, 'they were all men with silly moustaches and floppy hats. But Break has a point. We helped my dad out before and it worked, didn't it?'

No one disagreed.

'Not only did we do the right thing, but I for one had a load of fun. So, why not again? We make a good team.'

'But she made you fetch her coat!' said San.

'True. She's obviously used to getting her own way. That doesn't make what happened to her any fairer, though.' Charlie paused for a second. 'What was the stone worth?'

San had the figure imprinted on his brain. 'Over ten million dollars on a good day at auction. Oh, what gadgets the reward could buy.' He closed his eyes for a second and dreamed of a miniaturised, multi-functional heaven.

'Assuming we can actually pull it off!' Charlie wondered if, this time, they were in danger of taking on more than they could handle.

Ben stood up and pulled out his phone. 'There's only one way to find out. I'm gonna make the call. Yeah?'

There was no spitting on hands or signing in blood, but the deal was done. Ben punched in the numbers and the call was answered immediately.

'Ms Reliza? We'd like to take you up on your proposition!' The gang felt the adrenalin. There was homework to do, but not the sort that would show up in the school league tables.

*

'Looks like you're up to no good!'

Four heads turned. Break sighed. 'No, Baz. That's your department, I think.'

As usual, Baz had backup, and this took the form of some cavemen who had managed to make it all the way through to Year 10. Baz had taken the tie-shortening fashion to extremes, tying it so that only a fat stub showed, the rest tucked into his somewhat stained white shirt. In his left hand, carefully cupped, he held a cigarette.

'Fancy a puff? Oh, I forgot. Wimps don't smoke!'

'No, only people with a very low IQ do!' San muttered, still seething about what happened at the bowl a few days ago.

'Oh, I'm sorry. Little Musa had a bit of a fall. Accidents happen, don't they?' Baz sneered.

Break stood up. 'Was there something you wanted?'

This time, Baz wasn't scared. The boys behind him were raring to go. 'Only to smash your little skinny skater face in!'

'D'you know what, I've noticed that without your bike you tend to waddle!' said Break.

'What?' said Baz, with a puzzled look on his face. His associates began to close in. Their fists were not curling up in order to do some flower-arranging.

'Waddle, waddle, waddle!' mocked Break, even though he was about to be punched to kingdom come.

Charlie jumped up and ran between them. 'You'll have to hit me first!'

'I don't punch girls!' said Baz, as if he was discussing some finer point of honour.

'Then you won't mind if I remind you that the best form of defence is attack!'

'What?' said Baz again. All those words threatened to overwhelm him.

As his brain desperately tried to work out what she meant, Charlie leaped up gracefully and aimed her landing right onto Baz's left foot. Weight and gravity did the rest. He dropped his cigarette as he screamed in agony, chiming perfectly with the bell that rang out across the fields, drowning out the horrible noise.

The timing couldn't have been better, as various teachers spilled out onto the grass to summon their classes. The cavemen threw some vicious glances at the rest of the gang as they retreated behind their hopping leader. 'I'll...I'll get you later!' he shouted.

Charlie stubbed out Baz's cigarette. 'Dirty

habit! I did him a favour there!' She took a bow and skipped off to line up in her class.

Two days later, the group were standing outside a very solid-looking door, next to a shop in the heart of the jewellery district. The boys wore their school blazers so they would fit in. Even their shirts and ties were done up tight. It wasn't natural, yet the grown-ups in suits around them seemed to walk around like this all day.

'How'd she wangle this?' whispered San.

'Through an intermediary. Tirov & Sons already has links with local schools,' Ben replied. 'The head was only too pleased to let us come and visit for the day as long as he gets an article about it in the paper.'

'And it's a day off lessons for us. Cool!' Break was more than happy. 'All we need to do is act like schoolchildren...which we are!'

A voice came out of the grille, asking each of them to step in front of the video camera. With a hiss, the door swung open. Instead of a fancy shop filled with glittering displays, they were stuck in a small, shabby cubicle with another door in front of them. San tried to control his breathing. Small spaces were not his thing. Another camera whirred away above their heads.

The second door opened and led upstairs.

At the top stood a woman, eyeing them over. Her smile was smooth and her handshake formal.

'Welcome to Tirov & Sons! My name is Simone. Can I take your coats, please?' It was not a request, but a command. They handed them over. 'Do please take a seat. Mr Tirov will be with you shortly.' The final door she led them through revealed a cramped office. Simone's desk was clutter-free, surrounded by a bank of camera monitors that covered every aspect of the building, inside and out. They sat down on some very low black-leather sofas and stared at the pictures on the wall – coloured diamonds, blown up to look like huge Christmas baubles.

Five minutes later, a door at the back opened and Mr Tirov welcomed them into his room.

Break had been expecting opulence. But the room itself was small and practical, with a smallish white desk and books and cabinets lining one side. Mr Tirov sat down, indicating the seats which had been brought in to accommodate the visitors. He was a craggy old man, with wrinkles that looked like a plough had worked its away across his face. But his tanned skin, topped by a marvellous shock of white hair, indicated that age was no barrier to feeling alive.

'I am so glad to see some young people with enthusiasm for our little business. Where to start, I wonder?' He went on to talk about the birth of diamonds deep beneath the earth and the amazing volcanic action that moved them over millions of years towards the surface.

All this time, the boys took in their surroundings.

'Do you mind if I take notes?' asked San.

'Your interest honours me!' insisted Mr Tirov, little suspecting that, as he spoke, San was recording not his words, but the layout of the office. The man was a thief and they were here for one reason only.

Mr Tirov stood up and pulled one of the drawers open. Inside, there lay hundreds of small, folded paper parcels. He hummed to himself as he chose one and brought it to the table. He turned on a bright desklight and trained it onto the surface as he unfolded the parcel and let the stones spill out.

'Here you see how the stones look before we begin our work. Very little catches the eye, unless you know the signs.' He was right. The stones were dull-coloured, some shaped like octahedrons, others resembling featureless pebbles.

'But these…' Mr Tirov leaned over to pull out

another drawer lined with small, clear plastic boxes, 'are another matter!'

The boys were fascinated. There were diamonds of all shapes and sizes, each nestling on a bed of white foam, glittering and matching the shine in Mr Tirov's eyes. 'Now you understand, yes? Would you like to hold one? I find something special for you!'

Unbelievably, the man stood up and walked around and behind them to the safe in the corner, leaving three children in front of a table full of diamonds. Break let the thought cross his mind for an instant. It would take only a second for his hand to snake across the table. Their shininess pulled him in. He shook himself. *Don't be stupid. Then you'll be as bad as him!*

San was more interested in the safe. As Mr Tirov's back was turned, he quickly fired off some pictures with his mobile, zooming in on the safe's make, which was stamped in the top right corner. He slipped the phone back in his pocket.

'I bet that would be hard to break into!' San was already working out the angles.

'Bring me the person who could do so and I would shake him by the hand!' Tirov chuckled to himself. 'This safe is state-of-the-art and we have never had a break-in, though Mr Strassburger over the road has had three. There is even a joke going round that a man went up to my friend and said, "Mr Strassburger, I am so sorry to hear about your burglary...next Friday!"'

The three boys did their best to laugh. Their eyes lit up when Mr Tirov opened his palm to reveal a glittering sharp oval, clear and bright as if sunlight had been carved into a million reflections.

'Marquise cut, internally flawless, 15.05-carat...' He cradled the tiny stone as if it were a baby. 'And worth in the region of $1.2 million!'

'That's over half a million quid!' gasped San.

'Is this your most valuable stone?' Break asked.

'Ah, the greed of youth. There are always more precious pieces...' Mr Tirov slid easily away from a direct answer.

He let each of them hold the gem for a few seconds. Ben was the last to hold the diamond. He wondered if Mr Tirov could read his thoughts, and suddenly felt that everyone in the office was looking at him. His fingers fumbled and, next thing he knew, the stone tumbled out his hands and flew through the air towards the floor.

Mr Tirov's mouth fell open in shock. The change in mood was instantaneous. 'You stupid, blundering little fool!' he cried as he fell to his knees and began searching for the stone. The commotion caused Simone to pop her head round the door.

'Is everything alright?'

'It is now!' snapped Mr Tirov. He had found the stone hidden behind a table leg, quickly recovered it and put it away. 'You can close the door!' The anger in his voice pushed his secretary out.

'I'm really sorry!' Ben said, alarmed by Mr Tirov's reaction.

'It is no matter.' The old man had recovered his composure. 'Come, I will show you the polishing room.' He ushered them out quickly and began to walk down the corridor. Before they reached the end, they saw a set of stairs leading up into darkness.

'What's up there?' asked San.

'Attics, storage. No treasure, I'm afraid. But if anyone wanted to come down those stairs in the middle of the night, we'd have a lovely surprise for them!'

'What do you mean?' San was persistent.

'You know what they said about curiosity, boy?' Mr Tirov stared at him meaningfully.

San wondered about these threats. But as they traipsed past the stairs, his eyes took in several interesting features that could only be revealed in daylight. Good.

The rest of the afternoon passed in a blur as Mr Tirov handed them over to the polisher, who explained the process of turning unremarkable rocks into invaluable gems. San kept up with his notes. Finally, Mr Tirov passed them back to his secretary, smiled insincerely and closed his door.

Simone sat at her desk. 'It's not all glamour, I'm afraid. I've spent the last two hours on the phone trying to get the roofers back in. The last time it rained, it leaked right through the attic onto my desk!' She rolled her eyes as if a stain on a work surface was an actual crime. 'I hope you've learned lots about our business today. Is it something you could see yourselves getting into?'

Three heads nodded. Her words expressed their desires precisely. Simone reached under her desk with her left hand and the door swung open. They were free.

'Coming out tonight?' Break asked the others.

Ben was up for it but San shook his head. 'Busy,' he said.

Break looked at him. 'I've worked it out. Every Thursday for months now. What's happening?'

'Could be a secret girlfriend?' Ben liked the idea.

'Or a job at the local supermarket, saving up for gadgets?' Break suggested.

San was giving nothing away. 'Things to do, right. Can I go now?'

Without waiting for permission, he headed off in the opposite direction.

'Hmm...' said Break. He didn't like mysteries, but safes were easy compared to cracking open his inscrutable friend.

7. BREAKING SURF

Saturday 29 September, 4.13 am – back to the present

A people carrier drew up, tinted windows hiding the inside. It was as if they were expected. A back door opened and the man with the gun indicated for them to get in.

The normally bolshy Ben almost swallowed the diamond in fear. 'Who are...?'

'Do I look like the type of person who answers questions?' hissed the man. 'Get in!'

They did as they were told, the whole of the night's adventures and their hopes deflating in a second.

'Drive!' said the man.

In the darkened interior, they couldn't make out much about their new friend: jeans, tight

T-shirt showing tattooed muscles not be messed with. The inscribed doggies that snarled up and down the man's arms would never make loving pets. The man was also somewhat lacking in the hair department. The driver was similarly attired. Two thuggish peas in a pod. Stubblehead kept the gun trained on them, the car carefully observing the speed limit while turning down successive streets until the children had no idea where they were.

'Stealing is a crime,' said Stubblehead, as the car pulled to a halt. 'And you've got something that belongs to us!'

'No. I do believe we bought these boards fair and square. You don't look like skaters!' said Ben, helpfully.

The man turned round. In the corner of his left eye was a tattooed tear. Ben had a feeling Stubblehead hadn't cried in years. 'Oh, good. I like a boy with some fight in him. Torture is so boring, otherwise.' The man leaped out of the car and opened the back door as if he were a chauffeur. 'This way, ladies and gents. The fun is about to begin.'

The driver opened the door of what looked like an old industrial building. It was hard to see, as the council hadn't bothered repairing the few streetlamps that littered the lonely alley they were parked in.

Stubblehead prodded San with the gun. Real metal, cold on the skin. No reviews in *Gizmoid* magazine for this piece of kit. He pushed them into the darkness, threw a switch. A bare bulb revealed a corridor. It could be anywhere.

'You could, of course, hand it over now. It would save a lot of bother. But then my friend Johnny wouldn't be able to have his workout, and that would make him very unhappy.' Johnny – the driver – cracked his knuckles. A man whose hobby involved the breaking of bones. So this was what Baz wanted to be when he grew up.

Ben almost gave up at that point. He could have literally spat out the truth. Maybe they could all go home, uncover the lumps in their beds and practise their usual parental deception. But Stubblehead and his twin Johnny hadn't covered their faces. Once they had the goods, that meant the gang was no more than a loose end. And loose ends tend to get tied up.

'Tell you what. I need to make a call. I'll leave you to contemplate your less-than-rosy future. Oh, and let's do the health and safety thing first. You never know, we might strike lucky! Johnny?'

Johnny ambled over towards San.

'What have I done?' the boy whimpered.

But the hands that shot towards him were only interested in doing their job. He was expertly frisked and the fingers helpfully confiscated his keys. The others were searched in turn. Johnny quickly opened wallets and bags to empty them out. Nothing glittered. No treasure came to light, except for the drill, with its serrated edge glinting under the light.

Johnny passed the kit over to Stubblehead.

'Strange equipment for children to be carrying!' He felt the sharp edge of the diamond core. 'Very clever, very clever indeed. Looks like you've worked out some sort of silencer as well. What a pity...I could have used your skills. But the one object that really interests me appears to be...not here.'

The man shook his head. 'We always knew you'd have some interesting hiding place. It does make my job so much more pleasurable. Anyhow,' he said, as Johnny scooped up the kids' belongings and swept them into a canvas bag, 'I wouldn't want you to be making any calls while we're gone, summon the cavalry, ha ha!' Stubblehead obviously thought his joke was hilarious and Johnny joined in, though his high-pitched giggle made him sound like a hyena.

Finally, Johnny locked the door to the street and walked off to the other end of the corridor behind his boss, carrying the bag. A second door shut and the key grated in the lock. It was no better than a cage.

San panicked. 'They're not going to let us go! We are *so* dead!'

'I've worked that out, Gadget Boy!' snapped Ben. He paced up and down the lino floor. Maybe he could do a monkey kick on the front door?

Charlie was there before him. 'They've steel-lined the door. Last time I looked, you weren't black belt.'

'What about the other door?'

Charlie shook her head. 'Duh! Two very bad guys on the other side? Might be a teeny-weeny problem!'

'Point taken.' Ben sat down. It was late. Maybe San had been right. If only he were safe in his bed. 'Damn her! Why did Ms Reliza involve us in her problems? And how did this lot know where to find us? If it was Tirov's thugs, why didn't they surprise us in the building?'

'Questions aren't going to save our lives!' said San, miserably.

Ben felt his shoe vibrate. He pulled off his trainer and dug under the insole. 'You know, San, you might be a crackpot, but as a hiding place, it's not bad!' From a gap inside the foam layers, he pulled out his phone. He flipped it open and read the message. His face lit up. 'The evening's not over yet, folks!'

'What?' chorused San and Charlie.

'We're forgetting our lookout! And that's exactly what he's done – looked out for us. Break was about to join us when he saw the guy in the shadow and stepped back to watch. It was too late to warn us, but he managed to follow.'

'How does a board beat a car?' Charlie was intrigued.

'Dunno and don't care.' Ben was looking well pleased. 'Point is, he's watching the building. Tweedledum and Tweedledee are up on the first floor. And that, my friends, is our window of opportunity.' Ben pointed down the other end of the corridor, not at the door that looked as solid as the one behind them, but at the dusty rectangle of glass that lay above it.

'You are joking!' said Charlie.

'Never been more serious.'

From his perch on the rooftop, Break gazed at the figure with mounting despair. He felt like a spectator as a slow-motion accident unfolded. There were the gang, glowing with confidence as they exited Tirov & Sons with a very valuable package. And right behind them, a man moving out of the shadows, following them. They had no idea, clearly forgetting even the rudiments of caution. Success had gone to their heads.

Break fumbled with the keypad as his friends ran round the corner to pick up their boards. Damn! No signal. What was wrong with his stupid phone? If San was so clever, why hadn't he yet invented sound waves that weren't bothered by a few walls?

He only had seconds as he pounded down the stairs of the deserted building. The team were depending on him. At street level, he pushed off, willing his board to fly over concrete. He mustn't lose them.

Break turned a corner and put his foot down to slow his transport. A car stood, its idling engine covering the sound of Break's approach. This was even worse than he'd expected, as the blacked-out windows swallowed the others up. What now? How could a board beat a car?

Inspiration struck. If you can't beat them, join them! As far as the thugs in T-shirts knew, they had rounded up the whole gang. Good thing that counting was not their best talent, which meant that Break was invisible, to a degree.

The back door slammed shut and the man with

the gun didn't even bother looking behind him as he entered the passenger side.

Break took his cue and sped off down the tarmac, hoping that the driver wasn't too conscientious about looking in his mirrors. He crouched low and reached the back of the van just as it began to pull off. It was now or never. Break bent down and leant forwards to grab the metal trailer hook that poked out the back.

The car accelerated, almost separating Break from his board. The result would have been nasty, with the street becoming a giant skin-grater. Break held on for dear life. This was hitchhiking with attitude. He prayed for no unexpected manholes, focusing his mind on every bump. The first corner was the worst, as he was unexpectedly swung round and out, his wheels screeching in protest. He went with the flow, though the muscles in his arm complained loudly. This beat the bowl at the skatepark any day. For a moment, he even allowed the enjoyment to flood his veins as he surfed the sleeping streets and rode the tarmac waves.

Luckily for him, the car was observing the speed limit. But ten centimetres off the ground at thirty miles an hour felt like the Grand Prix. Finally, he felt the car slowing. It was time to let go. He uncurled his fingers and watched as the vehicle receded. Break stood up, ollied the kerb and dived into the nearest doorway, hoping the clatter of his board didn't echo round the street. His shoulder was on fire but that was the least of his worries.

As he turned, the car stopped and out stumbled Ben, San and Charlie, looking exhausted and frightened. The man with the gun paused to talk to them and Break caught sight of his face, illuminated by headlights. Where had he seen that tattoo before? Was it at Tirov's place? The diamond dealer's was hardly a tattoo parlour. Break shook his head, the memory gone.

A minute later, the gang was locked in the building. Break had to move fast. He ran to the door. Locked. There had to be a vantage point somewhere. He scouted the edge, trying to peer through the grime-covered windows. Finally, he found some old pallets to climb on. At the first floor window, a light came on. He scrabbled onto a ledge and peered in. It was an abandoned office. There was a single desk, its drawer hanging out like the tongue of a panting dog. One thug, looking bored, paced up and down the bare floor like a lion in a cage. Break was glad he was on the other side of the wall. The other thug was on his mobile, slumped in the only chair, with his elbows leaning on the desk. The smile on his face was easy to translate. He was no doubt speaking to Tirov, bragging about his catch and awaiting instructions. Break shivered as he remembered the look the old man gave Ben when he dropped the diamond.

Break jumped back down and thought for a second...the phone. They were in a signal area again! It was nice when the bad guys did you a favour. He began to text Ben. What he saw through the glass was a window of opportunity.

Ben had only ever seen it done once and that was in a movie. Probably wire-work with nice comfy crash pads and sugar-glass. There were no film cameras here. He walked to the door, counting his steps, and peered up at the glass. There was no time to rehearse the move. All he had was instinct and an understanding of angles. This was the true parkour moment.

'Could you please step out of the way?' San and Charlie shuffled back towards the street end of the corridor as Ben took several deep breaths to steady himself.

Come on, boy. He crouched down as if at the beginning of a race. It was now or never. He let his body take him, legs leaping off the ground as he sprinted down towards the other end, lungs pulling in the air to drive the pistons in his muscles. He was up to speed now, in the moment, as sure of this as he was of anything in his life.

He jinked slightly to the left, then swerved in a graceful curve in the other direction, his right leg stretched before him. His foot landed about half a metre up the wall. His leg bent to cushion the impact, creating the perfect jack-in-the-box. His body sprang off the right wall and his left foot connected this time. He was literally running side-to-side up the wall.

San watched in awe. This beat any computer game.

It was now all about aim. Ben's feet were missiles. They had to be going in the right direction or the local hospital would soon be running out of plaster. In a split second, his whole body shot forwards, feet first like an arrow. Bull's-eye! The window was a mere nuisance. It shattered and Ben flew straight through the frame into unknown territory – a boy with ten million dollars in his mouth.

It was a textbook move – the hand in the glove, the envelope in the slot, the body going where nobody was physically supposed to be. Ben was lucky. There were no filing cabinets with sharp metal edges to give him a cup of instant brain-squash. The bare floor reared up and bits of paper flew about in complaint as he hit the ground and rolled his way to standing position.

There was no time for applause. Ben only allowed himself one quick look back at the frame as he brushed the glass from his shoulders and picked a nasty shard from his bleeding cheek. His free-running mates would have been proud. It was a sick move and the second time this night he'd gone beyond the bounds of possibility. No one apart from the gang had seen it. Life was definitely not fair.

Brilliant! Johnny might have been an expert in body disassembly but his brain department was thankfully empty. The key was still in the door. Not only that, but the canvas bag containing their worldly goods sat on the floor like a gift. Ben scooped up the bag and unlocked the door, as his ears registered running footsteps. It was hard to camouflage the sound of breaking glass. Out of the pan and into the fire.

'Come on. We've gotta get out of here!' Ben turned to his right and ran, hoping that, for once, San's fear would give his legs some decent acceleration. Three teenagers against two overgrown nutters with guns inside a locked-down factory. The odds weren't good. They weren't good at all.

8. MISDIRECTION

Saturday 29 September, 4.41 am –
twenty–eight minutes later

'Give me your phone!' yelled San, out of breath.

'It's too late to call the Old Bill! Are you stupid?' Ben dragged San behind him. 'We have to find a way out.'

'Exactly. Trust me! And as for the "stupid" comment, I'll deal with that later.' They were running down yet another corridor where every door seemed locked. The footsteps were gaining on them. Any second now their pursuers would be in sight again.

Ben passed his phone over like the baton in a relay race.

'I hope Break is doing his job, or we're butcher's meat!' No one even had time to agree. Charlie kept hoping that one of the doors would give them an exit or, at the very least, a few seconds to hide and think. But this place was locked up tighter than the safe at Tirov & Sons. Ten metres ahead, the corridor dead-ended. They had a choice of four doors, two on either side. If they were like the others, then the gang were trapped.

San pressed away on the buttons, hoping he could run without looking where he was going. 'Got it!' The phone began to hum.

'What are you doing?' asked Charlie.

'Homing device. I downloaded the software onto all our phones ages ago, just in case...' San ran out of breath. 'Adapted it for mobile use. Break's phone is now the home station. Let's hope he got my message. All we gotta do now is follow directions!'

'It had better work!' muttered Ben. 'Trouble is catching up with us!'

At that moment, they heard shouts from the far end of the corridor. They were down to their last dregs of good luck. San gripped the phone tighter, willing it to be their techno saviour as he ran between each door. Suddenly, the humming turned into clicks.

'Here!' he shouted. The second door on their left. Charlie flicked the handle. It opened.

Ben spotted an old filing cabinet. It wasn't much, but might gain them a few seconds. He pulled with all his might and the heavyweight metal box toppled across the door. Thank goodness for antique furniture. Built to last and a nightmare to move.

There were stairs ahead of them. Upwards didn't seem like such a good idea, but the clicking phone insisted.

'What's he up to?' said Ben.

'No point asking!' Charlie ran up the steps two at a time and the others followed as fists and boots began battering the door behind them. Stubblehead's friend Johnny was not going to be in the best of moods if he caught them.

The steps wound round. From the fire doors on each floor it was obvious that these were the old emergency stairs. San paused for a second as the clicking stopped. The phone vibrated as a text came through.

'"Head for the roof!"' read San. It was crazy. He'd seen enough roofs to last him for ever.

Ben stubbed his toes several times. If it wasn't for the odd flicker of moonlight coming through broken windows, they would have been racing blind.

They were nearly done in. Up all night, and now this. They were running on empty. On the fifth floor, they finally came to a bolted door.

Stubblehead's voice floated up the stairwell, too near for comfort. 'Not too sure how you escaped the first time. But your sense of direction seems to have deserted you. There's no way out up there!'

They could hear the glee in his voice. This bloke really loved his job.

Ben pulled at the bolt. It hadn't been opened in years and rust had cemented it shut. 'Why won't the thing open?' He could feel the tears welling in his eyes. He thought of the twins, Mary and Grace, and his stressed-out mum. All gone. All for the sake of some dumb stunts and a pathetic code of honour which said that if your friend was in trouble, you helped them out. Now *they* were in trouble and who was there for them? The bolt was going nowhere. Neither were they.

Charlie pushed Ben out of the way, her dad's stories of breaking and entering revolving round her brain. He always told her to understand her adversary, whether it was a bully or a lock. There was no difference. In each case, you simply had to be prepared.

'What's the point?' snapped Ben as the footsteps pounded up from below.

'Give me a chance!' Charlie wiped the sweat from her face, pulled out a small can from her backpack and sprayed the bolt all over. She counted silently, one, two, three, as the liquid acid began to hiss and bubble, eating away the rust. Pulling her sleeve over her hand, she wiggled the bolt. As her dad always said, cleverness beat force most days. You had to use logic. This time, he was right. The bolt shot free.

'That's my girl!' said Ben, as he shouldered the half-height door open and they bent down to crawl through.

But success was tempered with despair. They were on a flat featureless rooftop in the middle of a sleeping and indifferent city. Ben ran round the edges to check. It was no good. Not another roof in jumping distance, and anyway, he couldn't leave the others behind. On the far wall, the roof gave way to a steep slate slope that slid towards the ground. Stubblehead was right. There was no way out. Break had let them down.

As if in agreement, the two men slowly climbed out of the roof doorway.

'Well done!' said Stubblehead. 'Me and Johnny here like a bit of exercise. You could call it a warm-up. Now, I strongly suggest you return what belongs to us, unless you'd like a free flying lesson?'

That was the problem. Whatever the outcome, this was one lesson that wasn't going to be cancelled.

9. ALL FOR ONE AND ONE FOR ALL

Saturday 29 September, 4.53 am – twelve minutes later

San, Charlie and Ben backed towards the edge of the roof as the two men advanced. They could only retreat so far. Then they were standing on the edge.

'I suppose it would be easier to search three dead bodies, Johnny? What do you think?'

Thinking wasn't part of Johnny's repertoire. All he managed was a grunt.

'I mean, this part of town, no neighbours peeking out from behind their curtains to report falling objects. But,' said Stubblehead in a coaxing voice, 'you give us the diamond and we'll all pretend this never happened. You'll be on your way home in a matter of minutes. Johnny here might be out of a job, but as I am an honourable man, I would rather see the return of what's rightfully ours and you tucked up safely in your beds.' Stubblehead waited for a response.

Ben noticed his tattooed eye was twitching. Stubblehead promising not to harm them? It was like asking a lion to give up meat for Lent. Not going to happen in a million years. He had to think, to stall the men.

He opened his mouth and poked out his tongue, letting the diamond fall into his upraised palm. 'Is this what you're talking about?'

Stubblehead's eyes glittered darker than any stone. 'Oh, yes!' He stepped forwards as if mesmerised. 'Oh, yes indeed. Not a bad hiding place, either. Hand it over, but do wipe it first. I've no desire to share your germs. There's a good boy!'

Ben didn't like the man's tone. He wasn't a dog with a stick. 'One step nearer, and I throw it!' He pulled his arm back.

Stubblehead reacted as if he'd been punched in the stomach. 'Whoa there. Easy does it!' For the first time, there was a flicker of fear in his eyes.

But what good would it do them? Buying a few seconds would make no difference in the end.

Down below in the alleyway, Break was making his last-minute calculations. He wasn't normally superstitious. Nevertheless, he crossed his fingers as he leaped off the end of a huge open skip at the side of the warehouse. He looked up towards the sky, just able to make out the rooftop. The sound of voices drifted down. They didn't have long now. He furiously punched the keys on his phone and pressed send. It was up to San now, to believe in him and do what he had to do.

San felt his pocket vibrate. He turned side on so that the men couldn't see and slipped out his phone. He read the text and, as the words sank in, glanced behind him.

'Ben. Do you trust me?' said San.

'This is no time to get soppy, San.' Ben was in a staring match with Stubblehead, the diamond loose in his sweaty fingers.

San moved closer, so that the men couldn't hear. 'Listen. Break joked about the musketeers.' He pointed behind them.

Any second now, Stubblehead and his colleague would rush them.

'My employer would be very unhappy if you threw away his stone!' Stubblehead and Johnny had split up now, and were circling the gang, closing in.

'Well,' said Ben, 'his happiness isn't really my concern.' He turned and winked at Charlie. San's message had well and truly got through. 'I'm afraid that we have another engagement, so we'll be saying goodbye!'

Before Stubblehead could register surprise, two things happened at once. Ben's hand flew back and threw the stone right towards and over them. Their heads swivelled, following the shining arc as ten million dollars landed near the door and rattled round the rooftop.

With their attention momentarily elsewhere, Ben grabbed hold of his friends' hands. The three of them turned round on the far edge of the roof and stepped off into nothing, screaming in unison: 'All for one and one for all!'

'Er, boss! They've gone!' said Johnny, tearing his eyes away from the spot where he thought the stone had landed and spying the empty ledge.

'I don't know why I employ you. Sometimes having such a dim-witted brother has its drawbacks!' Stubblehead ran to the edge of the roof and peered over to see a steep slate slope, now missing some of its tiles. He heard a loud crash, then silence. What were they thinking? It would be a messy clean-up, but that was Johnny's department. The thought of three dead kids came into his mind for an instant. He dismissed it. They had what they'd come for.

'Get the diamond!' said Stubblehead.

Johnny ran back towards the roof door and went down on his knees.

'It's dark, boss!'

'Use your lighter! If you see something that glitters, pick it up!'

'Oh…yeah.' Johnny flicked on the lighter and waved it over the area where he'd seen the diamond land. After a few seconds, he gave a cry: 'Got it! Er, boss?'

'What?' Stubblehead was tired.

Johnny stood up and walked slowly towards his brother, holding in his hand not the stolen diamond, but a small shard of glass.

'You idiot! We've been taken for a ride!' Stubblehead was tempted to take the shard and gouge D-U-M-B into his brother's forehead. Instead he pounded back towards the door and down the stairs three at a time.

Ben remembered the slide in his playground. One time, when he'd been about five, he'd thought of going down head first. It had seemed like a good idea. But the metal was as smooth as grease, so he'd shot down and off the end, his face scraping the so-called safety matting. His nose had erupted like a blood fountain as his mum came running. She'd told him off then – but what about now?

The three of them slid down the slate, accelerating with every second. There was no way this was going to end with a mere bloody nose. What was San thinking? This was so unlike him, literally to leap into the unknown. Charlie was holding tightly onto his arm, as if Ben were a magician, able to conjure a parachute out of his sleeve.

There was nothing to slow their descent, no way their feet could get even slight purchase on the tiles. The tiles agreed, coming away under them, slicing past them like Frisbees edged with razor blades. The screaming stopped. At this speed, it was hard even to breathe. Any second now and the slope would give way to a sheer drop. All their plans smashed to smithereens. Nought to sixty in three seconds flat and no brakes fitted.

The slope ended and three bodies tumbled out over the edge into freefall. No move in the gym could prepare for this.

San thought about all the gadgets he would never get to try and about his dad working long days and nights to look after him. Charlie felt she'd let her dad down. He'd gone on the straight and narrow, put prison behind him, and now look at his daughter! And Ben said his prayers as all their thoughts flew round like a flock of startled pigeons.

There was a loud *whoomp*! Three bodies hit something solid. But that something crumpled and gave way, cushioning their impact. There was silence.

Break ran to the side of the skip and clambered up. 'Anyone in there?' He tried to keep his voice jokey, scared of what he might find. No response. He looked over the edge to see a mountain of cardboard boxes, recently collapsed.

'Owww!' San was the first to come to. Every part of him ached. If this was heaven, it was a distinctly painful place and oddly filled with bits of brown cardboard. The others began to move. 'Are we…?'

'Alive? Yeah. I think so!' Charlie felt as if her whole body was about to turn into one big bruise. Stones were good at falling, but she wasn't. She slowly and gingerly began to climb out from what could have been a coffin. 'Where's Ben?'

'Here!' came a voice as Ben sprang up and smirked at Break. 'Now that was awesome!' Years of jumping had taught him to relax rather than tense up at the moment of landing. As far as he could make out, all his limbs were in working order. He was a human spring on legs. 'How did you know we'd make it?'

'I didn't...' said Break, with a frown. 'But the boxes looked good to go and we didn't exactly have weeks to come up with a plan. Any broken bones?'

Everyone shook their heads.

'Come on, then, I only bought us a few minutes while your new friends work out what's happened.' He helped each of them over the edge of the skip.

San was shaking all over, but the grin on his face told a different story. 'We should open this place up to the public! Charge them a fiver a go!'

'What, with broken legs thrown in for free?' Break ran ahead of them, round the side of the building to the people carrier. Within minutes, the tyres were let down and their skateboards retrieved through a smashed window.

'They really should watch out for vandals, you know!' smiled Ben as they set off into the night.

A minute later, the men ran out of the building. They paused for a second, trying to hear which way the kids had gone. But the sound of wheels on tarmac had already faded. They headed for the car. They would simply quarter the streets and catch up with them. When Stubblehead saw the tyres, he kicked the bonnet, hard. Then he kicked his brother even harder, desperate for someone to blame. At least, thanks to another member of his family, he knew where to find them. It was going to be difficult, but not impossible.

Half an hour later, the gang had reached the street corner where they usually split up. There was a slight chill in the air and the sky had turned musty grey. Dawn was on the way, and autumn was not far behind.

'Everyone alright?' asked Break.

'I'm tired, thirsty, bruised all over and I've nearly been killed. Apart from that, I'm fine!' said San. 'And we lost the diamond. So we've got nothing to show for it.'

Ben turned to his friends. 'I had to do it. To give us time.'

They all nodded. He was right, but that didn't make it any easier.

'Anyhow, who said we lost it?' Ben flicked out his tongue for the second time that night.

'Oh, you are brilliant!' said Charlie as the stone flared out under the neon streetlight.

'Let's have that in writing!' Ben took a bow but

not before Break tried to punch him on the shoulder for winding them up. 'Now, all we have to do is get the stone to my mum's friend.'

'...Coupled with the fact that Tirov's thugs will be watching her like a hawk.' Break was right. The situation was impossible. 'It's been a long night. Let's talk in the morning.' He stopped and looked at each of them in turn. 'And don't forget. We did this. No one else could have or would have!' With the pep talk over, he peeled away and headed down the street.

There were no goodbyes. They had to move quickly to slip home before early rising parents sussed them out.

Ben tucked the stone back under his tongue. It wasn't a safe, but it would do. He pushed off and click-clacked his way through the streets until he came to an alley that ran between two sets of back gardens. Other prowlers had also been out, as the ripped rubbish bags testified to the presence of hungry urban foxes. He came to a stop outside the back gate and carefully lifted the latch, stashing his board in the small shed and walking up the garden path. The key was where it should be, under the broken flowerpot.

A few seconds later, he was sneaking upstairs like a thief in his own house. He crept past his parents' room, hoping they were both asleep with baby Thomas tucked into his cot. He peered into the twins' room, the pale crescent-moon nightlight filling it with a soothing glow. Bunk beds squeezed up against the wall and the sisters out for the count as their twinkling-star mobile whirled above their heads.

He heard a sound behind him and dived into his room and under his duvet. A moment later, his mother's head poked round the door.

'Is that you, Ben?'

Ben's heart beat fast. 'Yeah, Mum. I...been to the loo.'

Her face creased, the eyelids still looking like the land of wakefulness was a trip too far. 'You don't normally wake up...' Her nose wrinkled. 'And what's that smell?'

Ben realised that the life-saving skip had been filled with more than cardboard. He stank. 'Dunno...'

'Boy, you're old enough to wash yourself. Can't get you no girl if you let them armpits go, huh? You be sure to have a shower when you get up!' His mum gave one more look around the room, now filled with early morning light. Finally, she sighed and closed the door.

Ben's heartbeat slowed to normal. The fight

went out of him. Before he felt exhaustion take over, he managed to extricate the cause of all their troubles and place the stone under his pillow.

It was a problem, but all he could do was sleep on it.

10. WORKING IT OUT

Saturday 29 September, 2.15 pm

From the outside, the place looked depressing: black grease on the drainpipes to stop unwelcome climbers, steel bars over grimy windows and steel-lined double doors worthy of Fort Knox. Inside was a different matter. The reception area was bright and filled with the perfume of fresh flowers. From behind another set of doors came the sound of sudden thumps that seemed to shake the whole building, followed by screams and shouting. The receptionist didn't even look up from her desk.

A woman pushed open the swing doors and strode out. She was dressed in a tight-fitting leotard and covered in sweat.

'Mrs Olatunji, the VAT forms have come in.'

The receptionist beckoned to a huge sheaf of papers.

The woman grabbed a towel from a rack and wiped her face, frowning as she peered at the mountain of paperwork. 'Why me?' she grimaced. 'That lot!' she pointed back at the doors. 'They don't realise that stunts never win prizes. Trying to teach them a routine is like trying to build a house out of jelly!' She strode off towards the showers. 'I'll deal with these later, Monica!'

Inside the hall, San sat with his PDA on a gym mat while his friends carried on their workout. The large, vaulted room was surrounded by climbing bars and the sprung wooden floor resounded to the moves made by Charlie, Ben and Break.

'I don't know how you lot have the energy!' San massaged his wrist, bent backwards in the fall from the roof.

'You should try it sometime!' Ben sprinted straight towards a wall. At the last minute, he ran straight up it as if he were a spider, then flipped over backwards, flying through the air as he turned to land on his feet. It was nothing compared to last night, but practice was practice.

'Try putting a corkscrew in that,' suggested Charlie.

Ben gave her a look.

'Alright. Leave it to the real gymnasts!' Charlie loped towards the same wall, but moved more elegantly as if its vertical surface was simply another dance floor. There was a smooth ease in the way she used the wall as a springboard to dive backwards and over. In mid-flight, she began to turn, twirling right round like spaghetti on a fork until she landed feet first and facing the direction she'd come from. Unlike Ben, her toes were tucked together.

Break clapped slowly as Ben scowled. 'We've got work to do, folks.'

They huddled together in a corner. The gym was a sanctuary. No bullies, no lessons and the perfect set-up to work out their moves.

Ben looked towards the door. 'My mum said she had some work to do. We should be alright for half an hour. By the way, was I the only one to land in something disgusting in that skip?'

'Oh, poor you!' said Charlie. 'Are you making an excuse for your BO?'

Ben stuck his tongue out at her, immediately reminding them of why they were here.

'What flavour is it?' asked San.

'Expensive flavour!' said Ben, dropping the diamond onto the mat, where it sat winking at them accusingly.

'We have to get rid of it!' said Break. 'And soon.'

'But Tirov's thugs won't rest until they've killed us, and our families and our hamsters!' San whined. 'How the hell did they know we were going to break in?'

'That's a good question.' Break thought for a second. 'Maybe there was a silent alarm. They didn't want the police to know that they'd nicked it in the first place, so a bit of quiet violence was called for. All I know is we have to deliver on our promise. The problem is that, by now, they'll have connected us to Ms Reliza. They'll be watching her.' Break paused. 'But... I have a plan.'

'I hope it's a good one!' said Charlie. 'One that involves us coming out of this with all our bits intact and still breathing.'

'Trust me. Your mate with no hair and the tattooed tear. Ring any bells?'

Everyone shook their heads.

'Never mind. Let's just say that a trip to the skatepark is overdue.'

'What, you want to shred your troubles away with a bit of concrete therapy? How does that sort our problems out?' said Charlie.

'Relax, Girl Wonder. My aim is to create a little diversion. Now, all we need is a visit to the costume jewellery department, courtesy of my older brother.'

'But I'm supposed to go to circus skills class this afternoon! We're doing fire-breathing today and I don't want to miss it! I've got all my kit ready to go.' Charlie pulled out her lighter and flicked it on and off to prove her point.

'Instant flames will have to wait. Do you want Stubblehead after you again?'

Charlie shook her head. There was no backing out now. The class would have to wait.

They trooped into reception.

Ben's mother came out of the changing rooms, towelling her hair.

'Where are you off to? I thought you'd only begun practice.'

'Sorry, Mrs O!' said Break. 'It's the sunshine. It makes me itchy for concrete!'

She eyeballed them all for a second. 'You're not up to anything, are you? It was trouble enough last time.'

Break acted his best. 'The only trouble is those BMXers at the park. It's like a war out there!'

'Hmm,' said Ben's mother. 'Well, you be careful, huh? No crash mats where you're going!'

She was closer to the truth than she realised. 'Don't stay out too late. Your father and I would like a quiet night for once. Oh, for a holiday!' she muttered, as she headed for her office.

The gang breathed a collective sigh of relief and made their escape.

Half an hour later, they trooped into the top-floor bedsit where Break's older brother, Lance, whiled away his hours while studying at uni.

Lance sat on the bed and listened to the story. In some ways, he was an older version of Break. Tall, thin and with the same floppy hair that had a natural aversion to shampoo. But there the comparisons ended. Lance was the less serious sibling. Instead of thinking about the meaning of life, he was more inclined to party his hours away and strut his stuff on any stage that would have him. Studying drama suited him perfectly.

'You want me to break into uni on a Saturday afternoon, when I've got to get ready for a date, and steal something almost worthless?'

'This might persuade you!' said Ben, doing his tongue-stud trick again.

'Oh!' said Lance, momentarily stunned. Acting was all about make-up and pretend. But this was the real thing. 'Oh!'

'Is that all you're gonna say?' Break looked at his watch.

'Easy does it, bro! It's not every day I have the opportunity to look ten million dollars in the eye!' Lance was practically drooling. His share of the reward would wipe out his student debt, and then some.

'So, can you help us?'

Lance leaped up from his bed, hangovers and thoughts of impending dates gone from his head. 'Sit tight. I'll be back in an hour. Can't offer you champagne while I'm gone, but help yourself to tea!' Lance crept out of the door like he was auditioning for a Bond movie.

'How did you ever wind up with him for a brother?' laughed Charlie.

Break declined to answer the question as he went off in search of hot drinks. He put on the kettle and found some teabags. But the bottled milk had a green ring at the top. Mould was not his favourite beverage. If this was what higher education had to offer, he was leaving school as soon as possible.

'Have you got a fix on Ms Reliza yet?' asked Break.

San tapped away on his fold-out wireless keyboard. But the screen on his PDA wasn't giving any satisfaction. 'Ringing her is out of the question. They'll have her line tapped, of course. I've tried online directories, figuring the business is in her name. Maybe she lives above the shop? She should have told us where to bring it!'

'That's what her number was for. She told us to memorise it and lose the card. If we got caught, she didn't want her information in our back pockets,' said Charlie.

'Alright for her!' muttered Break. 'Happy to leave us deep in the doo-doo...keep working at it!' He handed out three chipped mugs of scalding hot black tea. 'Excuse the china. My brother isn't known for his housekeeping skills. I think these cups were last washed back in the dark ages.'

San took a sip. 'Yurgh! That is foul stuff. Your brother needs help!'

'No,' said Break, 'we need his help.'

San studied the dark-coloured liquid. Inspiration struck. 'Brilliant! Who'd have thought your cuppa would save the day?'

The others turned and looked at San as if he were a few biccies short of a packet.

'Coloured tea...coloured stones. Ms Reliza said she specialised in fancy-coloured diamonds. Can't be many companies that do that. Let's see what my search engine makes of it.' San's fingers flew over the keyboard as if each digit was a top-class free-runner. 'Gotcha! Ms R. Eliza, purveyor of Fancy Coloured Stones to the Discerning Customer. It's a postbox address, but cracking that is child's play compared to the Chubb Sovereign.' His hands continued massaging the keys, urging them onto new discoveries. 'Here we are!' He pushed the screen round so that his friends could see.

Break talked them through the plan.

'Are you sure?' said Charlie, when he'd finished.

'No. But it's the best I can come up with.'

'Most people run away when they see a hornet. But you plan to walk into a hornets' nest... unarmed!'

'If you want to put it like that.'

Their conversation was interrupted by a slight scraping sound.

They looked up as the door handle began to turn. Lance couldn't have been that quick, surely?

San had been right all along. Tirov had also been doing his homework and waiting until they were all together again. Any second now, Stubblehead and his accomplice would walk in with triumphant smiles on their faces.

Break put his fingers to his lips. He crept towards the door, holding his skateboard in his right hand and slowly raising it up. It was multifunctional – both transport and hand-held weapon. Being smashed in the face by a set of gnarled-up trucks would at least give them a few moments' advantage. He tensed, ready to strike as the door swung slowly open.

11. HUNTED OR HUNTER?

**Saturday 29 September, 3.30 pm –
a few seconds later**

Break let out a howl that filled the room and alerted zoo-keepers on the other side of the city. At the same moment, he swung the board down and it landed with a sickening crunch on the hand that had appeared creeping round the edge.

There was an answering cry of pain. The kids leapt to their feet. There was nowhere to run, unless you counted a window with a freefall that led to no welcome cardboard boxes. They might as well go for it, take advantage before any guns appeared.

To their mixed dismay and relief, an unexpected sight greeted them as it writhed around on the grotty landing carpet. The only thing that flew out of the window was fear.

'Oh! Sorry!' said Break.

'Sorry?' cried Lance through gritted teeth, as he held his hand between his legs like an injured animal. 'Sorry? There must be a law against younger brothers attacking their elders. It's supposed to be the other way round!'

'Are you alright?' Break felt somewhat relieved he wasn't about to be killed.

'No.'

'The way you made your entrance...'

'OK! So I got a bit carried away. You know, the whole spy thing, creeping round. I was in my own private heist movie!' Lance wiped the tears from his eyes. His hand throbbed. He finally managed to uncurl his fingers and reveal the worthless piece of glittering junk that might save the day.

'Very nice indeed!' said Ben. 'Almost as if they were related to each other.' He pulled out the real diamond so that comparisons could be made. From a distance, which was all they needed, the bit of paste did its job beautifully.

Break nodded. They'd used fakes before. It had worked well back then. If it ain't broke, don't fix it. 'Cheers, bro. Stick your hand in some ice. Time to go!' With barely a backwards glance, Break scooped up the fake and headed down the stairs, followed by the others.

Charlie lingered for a moment. 'You know Break...always onto the next thing. He does care about you.'

'Sure.'

'Will you be alright?'

Lance wiggled his fingers. 'Nothing broken, I hope. But they won't be using me in any hand-cream adverts for the next few weeks! Anyhow, it's you lot I'm worried about. My brother annoys the hell out of me, but he's the only one I've got.'

'Break's alright. He knows what he's doing. Thanks, Lance. See you later.' As she ran down the stairs, Charlie thought about his comments. He was right to be worried.

As Lance stuck his hand in the freezer, the gang skated to the bus stop and waited.

Ten minutes later, they were riding on the top deck. The sky was overcast and muggy. Weird summer weather, like a storm was about to burst over the city. Break loved it when the bus brushed past the trees, as if there was a private green world up there, despite all the pollution. They stopped at a set of roadwork traffic lights. On the pavement, people walking made quicker progress than the snarl-up of cars, buses and lorries.

‘Check it out!’ said Break.

They leaned over their seats and looked down into an enormous, concrete-lined pit by the side of the road. The diggers were empty, standing like huge metallic beetles, shut down for the weekend. The pit led onto a tunnel that must have been at least seven metres high, its big black mouth swallowing up the darkness.

‘Storm outflow. All these heavy storms, thanks to global warming. The rain’s gotta go somewhere and the city doesn’t want that to be people’s basements.’

‘Never knew you were interested in civil engineering,’ said San.

‘You are entirely missing the point, Gadget Boy. That there concrete is aching to be ridden and only the most talented of our crew can carry it off!’

The others turned away. When Break began to brag, it was time to plug in the iPods.

Once they reached their stop, the gang alighted and scooted off in the direction of the park. Another busy afternoon, with the skaters queuing to drop the bowl. For once, they weren’t here to skate but to act as bait.

‘Play at being normal!’ muttered Break as they walked through the wire-mesh gate.

'What, like teenage skaters?' said Ben. 'But we are.'

'Yeah, yeah.' Break scanned the mix of surf-wear, baggy shorts and Goth outfits. The variety of piercings was mind-boggling. Finally, his eyes spied their target. 'Spot on. I knew I was right.' He edged unobtrusively in the direction of the bowl, checking his trucks and bearings as if getting ready to carve up the vert. It was like being a conman. He was searching for someone who would be searching for him. But that someone wouldn't figure it out in a million years. This was Break's advantage. Knowledge. The best weapon of all.

He stood at the edge of the bowl, pretending that all the other skaters were too fast for him to get a ride. He waited. Five minutes. Then the familiar voice.

'Thought I'd find you here!'

'Wow! What a brain. A skater goes to a skatepark! How did you work that out?'

Baz ignored the insult. 'You're in too deep this time!' he snarled. His bike looked as polished as ever, compared to Break's beaten-up board, with the trucks looking like they'd been gnawed by a particularly ferocious hamster.

'I don't know what you're talking about.' Break

was enjoying this. Lance had given him some tips. This was far more fun than any stage.

'The question is, which one of you has got it?'

'Well, me, obviously. If by *it*, you mean talent? Or...' Break pulled Lance's prop out of his pocket. '...Or this?' His move was subtle enough that no one else noticed the glittering trick that lay in his hand. It was for Baz's eyes only.

The smile on Baz's face curved like a sharpened scythe. His pudgy fingers almost made a grab for the goods. But one look at Break's face said that such spoils would not be won easily. 'Your choice!' said Baz, as he looked away into the distance and gave the thumbs up.

'Exactly!' said Break, following the line of Baz's gaze as it travelled outside the park into the street, where two huge black trail bikes waited, their powerful engines merely murmuring. Break wondered for a second about families. Was there a whole line of Bazes going back through history, all of them pin-eyed skinheads, genetically bred for the mashing up of innocent bodies? It didn't bear thinking about. Time to play.

He ran past Baz, pausing only to wink at Ben and the others. The bikes, ridden by Baz senior (aka Stubblehead aka Dez Jenkins) and brother

Johnny, were idling on the other side of the square. One of them was murmuring into his mobile. It gave Break time to hit the entrance and push off down the road.

The bike engines screeched into life, their rumbling turning into a throaty roar. At least they wouldn't use guns out here in public. He hoped. All he had to do was put some serious distance between them. He didn't have long. Footpower had little chance against 750cc of streamlined engineering. Break slalomed between surprised pedestrians, a couple of whom decided instantly to complain to the police about the state of the nation's youth. He hoped the council had kept up with their repairs, as a sudden pot-hole might mean him headbutting solid slabs. Instant tooth-loss did not appeal.

At least he was on a hill. He used the gradient to build up speed as the bikes zipped down the road, catching up way too quickly. Speed cameras flashed like distress flares, but even Break could spot that the black bikes, topped by men in black leather with mirrored helmets, had blacked-out licence plates. So black was the new black... He guessed it was a fashion thing.

They were parallel to him now and he could see

one of the bikes slowing, ready to execute a perfect pincer movement, one behind, one in front and him clamped between as the jaws began to close. Passers-by jumped out of their way and averted their eyes. There was one thing you could rely on with the London public: they knew better than to interfere. Community spirit had passed its sell-by date years ago. No help there, then.

The roadwork traffic lights were stuck on red. It was no problem for the motorbikes. They simply cut across the road and mounted the pavement, now within metres of Break.

Break watched the orange netting and 'keep-out' signs of the building site slide past. He could smell the fumes from oversized bike exhausts and feel two pairs of eyes drilling into him. In a few moments, it would be more than just eyes.

It was now or never. He hated being goofy-footed. It was one trait he'd inherited from his old-school dad. But with boards these days, built to go either way, it didn't really matter. Best to ride in your comfort zone.

He shifted slighty to the front of his board, preparing his left foot. As he must have been travelling at well over forty miles an hour, any wrong move now would be disastrous. The bikes closed on him. A leather-clad arm reached out to grab him but only came up with air.

Break bent his knees and punched down on the nose of the board. At this speed, he might as well have been confetti. The board bounced off the pavement and Break crouched as he surfed some invisible wave, arcing over the building-site netting as the board flipped round and over. Nollie-twist. If Ben and Charlie could do their moves, why not him?

If he thought the bikers would be put off, he was wrong. The plastic netting surrounding the site was way too flimsy for a pair of charged-up superbikes. Their grippy front tyres shredded it like paper.

Break was too busy to look behind him as he began his descent. It always amazed him when he pulled any trick how the board seemed to be attached to his feet with elastic. In midair, his body and board could be divorced, doing their own thing, yet somehow, on landing, the relationship was almost always repaired. Reunion was the goal. This time was no different, as he thumped back onto the deck and sped down the steep slope of the concrete pit. Made it.

His self-congratulation was short-lived as he stole a glance behind him in time to see two bikes leap over the edge and join him on the steep downhill gradient. The tunnel mouth loomed in front of him like a giant, filled-in O. Down here, away from pedestrians, his pursuers might not feel so restrained. His shoulders itched as he imagined being lined up in their sights. Bikes without engines, no problem. But these two thundering beasts were topped off by men with guns – guns loaded with bullets more than happy to break all known speed limits.

Break shuddered, both from the vibrations as the board zoomed over the newly minted concrete towards the tunnel, and at the realisation that his so-called plan was rapidly unravelling.

12. FULL CIRCLE

Saturday 29 September, 4.41 pm – meanwhile

Baz had no desire to miss out on the fun. He hared off out of the park on his bike, dreaming of the motorized version. When he grew up, he wanted to be like Daddy. His future sorted, he vanished down the hill, puffing to keep up with the chase.

Ben rolled the stone round in his mouth and gave the others a big, cheesy grin. 'We've bought ourselves a whole load of time – let's return this to its rightful owner...'

'And if you're not thinking about the reward, then my name is Prince Charles!' said Charlie.

'Name's right, but as for royalty?' Ben sucked his teeth.

'What about Break?' San asked. 'We've fed

him to the wolves!'

'I'm sure he'll be fine!' said Charlie. But Lance's words hovered in the air. She shook her head and tried not to imagine what could go wrong. Break was fast, but was he fast enough?

Ben didn't bother looking back. Bowl-riding was the last thing on his mind. A bus and tube ride later and they entered a part of town that screamed *wealth*. Black-painted doors and huge Georgian windows hinted at lives beyond any they could even dream of.

San checked his PDA and looked round. 'This is it.'

They walked up a set of immaculate stone steps. Two manicured bay trees in zinc pots stood either side of the door. On the wall was a discreet brass plaque: 'R. Eliza – The Finest Fancy-Coloured Stones'

They stood there, aware of their clothes and boards, aware that in no way did they fit in.

'Here goes!' said Ben, lifting the knocker, which was in the shape of a golden lion's head with two glittering eyes.

The resulting boom echoed down an inside passage. They waited. Ben wanted to see the look on Aunty R's face when she saw them. It would make her day.

A few seconds later, the door swung open, as if blown by the perfume that wafted out. Ms Reliza stood there. Slinky black dress, black tights, black stilettos, dyed black hair. She was a vision.

Ben gulped. Normally, he had no problem talking. The only problem he had was shutting up. He really had to get a grip. 'Ms Reliza!' he began.

Before Ben could continue, Ms Reliza looked up and down the street and motioned them inside. 'I thought you might find me. Quick. Quick! Did anyone see you?'

'No,' said Ben. They stood inside a long, wood-panelled corridor. It was dimly lit.

Ms Reliza opened a door, revealing an old-fashioned office that looked more like a library, lined floor to ceiling with books. She strode to a leather-covered desk and sat down on the other side. She indicated for them to sit down.

Charlie felt like she was in a business meeting. A bit of gratitude would have been nice.

'We couldn't ring. Tirov's men found us out. We don't know how!' explained San. 'They probably tapped your phone.'

'Ah!' said Ms Reliza. 'Of course...Tirov's men... You really are good.'

Ben smiled. 'We do our best!'

'Which means, I assume, that you succeeded?'

Her glossy red lips trembled with anticipation. 'But you have it, yes?'

Ben opened his mouth and spilled the beans. The stone lay on the table between them. A leaf that decomposed and became coal. A piece of black grit compressed through eternity until the fire hidden inside was revealed.

'My baby!' Ms Reliza cooed. Her hand slipped towards it, cautiously, as if the fingers couldn't quite believe the message passed on by the eyes. She looked in wonder at the teenagers. 'You really did it!'

'We did!' snapped Charlie. 'And almost lost our lives in the process. We've been nearly arrested, chased, locked up, threatened with torture and worse, survived a four-storey slide and left our best friend in who-knows-what danger...'

'Charlie's right!' interrupted Ben. 'The problem is Mr Tirov. He knows we took it and I don't think he's a happy bunny. His employees are something else altogether.'

'Yes, they are,' sighed Ms Reliza as she cradled the diamond. 'But the problem is, I think, yours.'

They looked puzzled.

'What do you mean?' said Ben.

'Oh, dear. I do wish it hadn't come to this! You should have handed the diamond over last night!'

'But what was the point of that? We'd be back to square one. And they weren't exactly going to let us go!' Why she was talking like this?

'Yes. Those men can be a bit...enthusiastic. Still. All's well that ends well! But I do need to know, Benjamin. You haven't worried your mother with any of this?'

'Nah! Course not. She'd ground me for months. Her idea of danger is for me to do a double flip rather than a single. And with a nice soft crash mat to land on.'

'Good! Now what am I going to do with you three?' The change in her tone was unmistakable.

The table was suddenly bare of its treasure. Ben, San and Charlie found themselves looking directly into the mouth of a gun, held by the very firm hand of Ms Reliza.

Break was travelling at a phenomenal pace. He hoped his trucks were tight enough. The last thing he needed was a case of the speed wobbles. There was a soft pinging sound. He looked ahead of him and saw a small puff of dust as a chip of concrete flew up. More bullets ricocheted around him as he dropped down the steep slope towards the tunnel. What weapon did he have? Only cunning and street skills. Let's see.

The great Bob Burnquist had done some stunts in his time. The man built a ramp over the Grand Canyon with a rail that jutted out into the ether. He dropped the ramp on his board, accelerated down to finally pop the lip to grind the rail. There was a thousand-metre drop on the other side. The board left his company, and luckily the parachute opened in time. It was one wild move – the biggest air in history. But one of his other mad moments gave Break inspiration. It was said that only a few people worldwide had done it, all Americans. It was time for the Brits to earn back some ground.

Break hunched down, not sure he had enough velocity. He'd ridden some pipes in his time, hitting 10 or even 11 o'clock sometimes. But what he contemplated now was off the timescale entirely. The bearings did their work, spinning him up the other side. Let's see the bikers follow this! He reared up towards the vert and was suddenly over it, defying gravity – 9 o'clock, 10, 11. This was the point where the laws of physics dictated he should drop. But his nickname was Break for a reason, as rules were made to be bent and finally snapped.

As he blinked his eyes, he was upside down, his wheels still glued to the pipe. He was in the vortex now. It was the opposite of a rush – everything slowed down as Break and the board catapulted round. Again he blinked and it was nearly over as he rushed down the other side and into the depths of the tunnel. He'd done it! A perfect, full three-sixty revolution.

One of the bikes tried to follow him. Break had no idea what was happening, but his senses were sharp enough to feel the closeness of pursuit.

It was Johnny. A pretty good rider most of the time, but his eagerness to get hold of this annoying little brat and tear him limb from limb was his undoing. He gunned the bike up the side of the tunnel, pushing the throttle up to full power. The bike was willing, but at the critical moment, the engine miscalculated. Unfortunately for Johnny, that moment was when he was upside down.

The bike was simply too heavy. And the steroids Johnny took to pump his body up to almost twice its normal weight didn't help either. It was time for the game of consequences. Instead of looping the loop, Johnny fell straight down. To make matters worse, his bike descended with him, only this time he was underneath it.

Break registered the unhealthy crunching

sound as it echoed round the tunnel. There was an unpleasant scream, followed by silence. One down, perhaps permanently. One less Jenkins in the world had to be a good start. He heard the second engine roar. He wasn't out of the woods yet. He focused on the board, zipping from side to side, carving the tunnel like a speedboat on a river, trying to build up speed and hoping for the dim light to reveal a way out.

13. TIGHT CORNERS

Saturday 29 September, 5.23 pm – a few seconds later

'Yes. What am I going to do with you three?' The gun didn't waver; the manicured hand that held it was firm as a rock. The smile had long gone from Ms Reliza's face.

'Glock 18C, Machine Pistol. Nine millimetre! That's rare...' said San without thinking.

'Well done, young Mr Musa!' Ms Reliza nodded her head in acknowledgement. 'And, as you have no doubt worked out, capable of firing enough rounds in one burst to...how should I put it?... deal with more than one assailant.'

Ben stood up. 'What's going on?'

'Sit down!' she hissed.

He did as he was told, watching the barrel of

the gun as if it were a snake's head about to strike. 'But you're...'

'Not what I seem, I'm afraid. Sorry about all those little lies. They were necessary, you know.' The glossy lips screwed up in a grimace. All pretence of friendliness vanished.

'I don't believe this!' Ben stared at the woman who'd bought him chocolates as a child, who'd hung out at the shopping arcade with his mum, who'd been loyal when it counted. Who was she now?

'Let me tell you a story about a little girl who loved diamonds. She always thought that if she worked hard, very hard in this man's world, she might find a way to make her dreams come true.'

'Yeah?' said Ben. 'So what's all this then?' He swept his arm round the palatial office.

'Patience, Benjamin. You were always in such a rush! That's why your hobby suits you. Free-running...hmmm.' Ms Reliza leant over to stroke his cheeks, as Ben squirmed away.

San and Charlie were frozen to their chairs. It was all going horribly wrong.

Ms Reliza continued, as if she were desperate to explain, to justify. 'This little girl grew up. She worked hard – every hour under the jewel-like sun. But the margins, oh the margins! If you think each stone is worth a fortune – what about the work involved to make it desirable – buying, cutting, polishing, premises…?' She shook her head. 'The mortgage grew like a monster. All this' – and she too looked round the office – 'is built on the quicksand of a loan. The banks loved me at first, but what chance does a woman have? They gave me a month to pay them back or they would close me down. I had nowhere to go! My reputation would have been polished down to nothing!'

'But the diamond?' said Ben. 'That's why you took the risk!'

San looked at Ben. His mate still hadn't worked it out.

'No. The risk I took was much cleverer. Dear Mr Tirov did all the work for me, in a way. He bought the stone himself, cut it, and created treasure out of rock. But I was the one who heard about this stone and saw its true potential…'

'To steal it for yourself!' Charlie was fuming. All this and they'd been betrayed from the start.

'Not for me to steal it, sweetie! That was where my plan really shone! If you stole it and got caught, whose word would they take, with your reputation?'

'My mum trusted you!' Ben was flabbergasted. 'All those years ago, you stuck up for her. What happened?'

'People change, Benjamin.'

Ben frowned in disgust. 'Yeah. For sure. But this is so dumb. You were going to get the diamond whatever. So why the setup with your pet thugs?' It didn't make sense.

'Oh, I had to cut the line between all of you and myself. That way, I could become…untraceable. I simply needed your skills to break into that building and that safe. It was your rather reckless escape from a certain rooftop which made me alter my strategy. In fact, if you'd handed it over in the first place, we could have all been sleeping soundly tonight.'

'Yeah, sure. All we did was try to help you out. You've got your precious baby. What more do you want?' Ben asked. 'Can we go home now? And tell you what, why don't you ring your brainless employees and get them to lay off Break?'

'You make it sound so simple! Call off the dogs and everyone lives happily ever after!' Ms Reliza clicked off the gun's safety lever and screwed on a silencer as they watched in horrified fascination. 'On Monday morning, Mr Tirov will discover that his safe has been broken into. The police will be called and the papers shall have a field day. By then, you would have worked out that my story was full of holes. Tirov will want explanations, ones that I would not like *you* to give. What a pity it has to end like this. I have had to work overtime to put my plans back on track.

'After Dez informed me of your escape, I wasn't too sure if you had already worked out my... involvement. I took out some insurance, just in case.' Ms Reliza smiled.

'What do you mean?' Ben and the others were confused.

'It doesn't matter now that you're here. In fact, your arrival is quite perfect. Naturally, you are the main suspects. The papers will love blathering on about adolescent criminality while I shall board a plane to...somewhere else and begin to live the life that such a delightful gem will afford me.'

San worked it out. 'Which means that we're in the way.'

'Exactly.'

'But we're kids!' cried Charlie.

'Oh, my dear. Haven't you heard of conflict diamonds? The word "conflict" is there for a reason. I trust my employees won't have any problems chasing down a fourteen-year-old skateboarder. Meanwhile, I shall make sure you don't go blabbing a bunch of ill-informed truths to the police.' Ms Reliza's heart was colder than any stone. She levelled the gun and prepared to end three careers before they had even begun.

The shout echoed round the tunnel.

'You did my brother!' it screamed. 'Now I'm gonna do you!' Baz's dad gunned his engines. Out-tricked by a skateboard? Not for much longer.

Break felt the sweat in the hollow of his back, his T-shirt stuck to clammy skin. His thigh muscles ached from pumping the concrete. He couldn't keep this up. The light was also going as he headed into the tunnel's depths. Any advantage he had built up speedwise was being eroded. In the dark, no one would notice a dead Year 9 student.

Dez decided that the gun was too easy. His bike was built like a battering ram. It was a point of honour that he dealt with this brat personally, for the sake of his brother. A tattooed eye for an eye. All he wanted was to hear the sound of bones compressing, bending, snapping as the wheels ripped into his victim's body. Then the boy could be left to the rats and for the storm overflow to wash him away.

Annoyingly, the boy was weaving from side to side like a buzzing gnat. It was hard to aim his machine. Damn him! Didn't he realise it was over?

Break's eyes rolled round in his head like a fruit machine turning, desperately looking for a way out. Surely the engineers had built this trap with an escape hatch? The gangway, when he finally spotted it, appeared like a gift from the gods: steep steps heading up the curve and giving onto a short mesh platform with a half-height door. But there was a problem. If he ditched the board and ran up the stairs, he'd be a sitting duck, squarely in Dez's sights. His hatch to freedom was also a bullet-riddled dead end. There had to be another way.

Maybe he could ride it? He was already carving the tunnel up to the vert on either side. He'd have to time it right. There was only one go at this. He carved up the opposite side of the stairs, hitting 10 o'clock and turning backside. Now he bent his knees and pumped for all he was worth, willing his body to be a bullet, as he shot into the bottom of the tunnel. Then he was up the other side, and veering to the right of the stairs.

Dez hit the brakes, hard, and skidded to a halt. What was the kid up to? He pulled out his gun, though the boy moved too fast for him to get a shot. Dez watched in disbelief as Break rode right over the top of the stairs and then, in one fluid motion, kicked back on his tail and began plummeting down. The smile that had been absent from Dez's lips returned. Crazy boy was about to come down to earth. Or rather, steel-reinforced concrete with no give. If the drop didn't finish him, Dez was happy to pile in and complete the job.

Climbers on overhangs had ropes and pitons. Break had nothing but instinct, which told him the moment to see what his board was capable of had arrived. He was almost upside down when he leaned frontside and popped the tail. Flying squirrels would have applauded. But not yet. It wasn't like he could see where he was going. Oh, for eyes in the back of his head! The fall was way too fast as his weight carried him down. If he missed by a centimetre, his back would hit the stair rail. He could almost hear the snap, see the wheelchair, mourn the end of his skating days.

But the board, like a dog, remained faithful, guiding him through the currents of stale tunnel air. Odds were made to be defied and that's what

Break did as he crashed onto the mesh platform while Dez watched in uncomprehending shock.

Break's landing was far from perfect. But considering he'd just jumped backwards off an overhang, it was a miracle that he still had functioning ankles. Maybe rubber bones were a family trait. Break had never been so glad to see a door without a lock in his life. There was no pause in his motion. He leant forwards to push the handle down with one hand while gripping the board with the other. As he somersaulted through the opening, he heard bullets bouncing off the mesh, their echoes dying away down the tunnel. Close was not the word.

Light filtered in from above, sending down fingers of hope. He could just make out another ladder straight in front of him. No time for a breather. He ran up the ladder and pushed on the metal grating with the last of his strength. London air. Full of fumes. But right now, that smoggy stuff was sweeter than any milkshake. As he emerged out of the depths onto the pavement, a toddler in a pushchair screamed. The child knew all about monsters under the bed, but a mop-headed sweating beast emerging from the pathway? The mother gave Break a dirty look and swerved round him.

Dez threw his gun to the ground in disgust. In full leathers, he'd have no time to catch up with his quarry. And by the time he exited the tunnel and hit the road again, the boy would no doubt have vanished like a rabbit down the proverbial hole. He'd gone and so had the diamond.

At that moment, Baz came pedalling down the tunnel at full pelt, desperate to be in on the action. 'Uncle John's leg is in a funny shape. I've rung the ambulance. Did you get him, Dad?'

Dez looked round the empty tunnel, then grabbed his son by his ear and dragged him off the bike. 'What do you think, eh?' He couldn't work out what was worse, losing ten million dollars or having not one but two morons who were supposedly related to him.

14. CIRCUS SKILLS

**Saturday 29 September, 5.40 pm –
a few seconds later**

'Do you mind if I have a drink?' Charlie asked.

The gun didn't move. 'A drink? Or some secret weapon that your gadget-obsessed boyfriend has come up with?'

San went red as Charlie motioned to her bag on the floor. 'It's a bottle of water. Have a look yourself.'

'Well…' said Ms Reliza. 'We must accede to the last wish of the condemned, I suppose. You won't be thirsty where you're going. But I am not totally heartless!'

Ben looked at the hard-faced piece of work sat in the chair behind the desk. She was dead wrong on that score.

'Kick it over and don't try anything. My training was harsh, and this finger of mine is very, very fast.' Her glossy eyelashes indicated Charlie to get on with it.

Charlie shoved the bag with her foot, licking her lips as if they hadn't tasted liquid in days.

Ms Reliza leant forwards, carefully keeping aim with one hand as she rifled through the bag's contents with the other. The offending plastic bottle was removed and held up to the light. 'Looks harmless enough to me. Have a drink, then!' She threw the bottle to the girl. 'It's going to be your last.'

For once, Ms Reliza's perfume worked against her, camouflaging the smell as Charlie hoped it would.

Charlie took a long, hard swig from the bottle, noticing the satisfied look in the woman's eyes. *Not for much longer*, she thought.

Ms Reliza's trigger finger might have been fast, but she was up against a girl who'd been studying circus skills since the age of three. The trick with audiences was always to surprise them. Open a curtain and there's a lion. Close it. Open it again – a hundred doves fly out of empty space.

This time, it wasn't a curtain that opened and closed, and the audience was somewhat smaller, but Charlie didn't mind. She swilled the liquid round her mouth with no intention of swallowing.

The moment Ben saw her take the drink, he'd been with her. What Charlie needed was a distraction. 'Listen, Ms Reliza, there must be a way we can work this out!' Ben leant forwards, trying to persuade.

It was enough. The gun and Ms Reliza's eyes flicked towards the boy. 'Conversation time is over!' she hissed.

It was all Charlie needed, the magician's pause while the audience momentarily looked elsewhere. All sleight of hand was based on this. Vision could not be in two places at once. She slipped the lighter out of her hand and flicked it on as she opened her mouth.

Ms Reliza was quick. The moment she realised what was happening, she began to swing the gun towards Charlie and depress the trigger.

Out of Charlie's lips came an angry roar. The liquid ignited instantaneously, sending a funnel of flame straight towards Ms Reliza, blocking her view as the gun fired wildly. Charlie Cooper, the original human flame-thrower.

The flare was fast, and greedy. The huge amount of expensive, alcohol-based spray that

Ms Reliza used to keep her hair straight was an added bonus. The woman's head erupted like a fireball.

Several bullets thudded into the wall. A Chinese vase that had survived four centuries of handling shattered into irreparable pieces. Fifteen thousand pounds lost in a single second. Charlie didn't even feel the one bullet that grazed her shoulder as she watched Ms Reliza scream and drop the gun.

Ben dived for the weapon as Charlie felt her humane instincts kick in, despite her desire to leave the woman to burn in hell. She pulled off her jacket and jumped onto the desk and over to land by the chair, and threw it over Ms Reliza's head, holding the cloth tight for a couple of seconds to quell the flames. Her jacket would be ruined, and as for what lay underneath? She paused and the burning sensation high up on her own left arm hit home. Charlie looked over to see blood welling out of the furrow dug into her skin.

Ms Reliza coughed heavily as Charlie pulled off her coat. San and Ben smiled grimly. They said that beauty was only skin deep. It was true – the mask of glamour had been burnt away. Her hair had been turned to black frizz and her eyebrows more than trimmed. Smoke still rose from her head, as if Ms Reliza were no more than a recently extinguished cigarette. Aside from that, the woman was dead lucky. She might be prematurely bald, but the flames hadn't had time to burn her skin.

'Having a bad hair day never killed anyone,' said Ben as he reached over to the top desk drawer and pulled it open, keeping the gun carefully aimed as he rifled through the contents. 'First, we'll take this back and return it to its rightful owner. Say goodbye to your love and joy, Ms Reliza.' Ben wiped the stone, as if her fingers were dirtier than any saliva, and popped it back in his mouth. 'Charlie, you need to get that graze seen to!'

'I'll be fine!' Charlie was now using her coat to staunch the flow of blood. 'It's my jacket I'm worried about!' She gritted her teeth against the pain.

'And what have you got to smile about?' Ben looked at Ms Reliza's face as it cracked up in a sooty grin.

'Oh, plenty. Bravo on the performance by the way.' She nodded towards Charlie as if acknowledging another warrior's superior skill. 'I've heard that you always find your way out of a tight corner. But I think I'll have that stone back now, if you please!' She combed the remains of her hair over her shoulders as if that would make her look more presentable.

'You're joking, woman!'

'No. Never been more serious.' She turned to Ben. 'I mentioned insurance earlier. Ask your computer friend about the importance of back-up. He'll tell you. My instincts about your talents were right. As soon as I heard you had escaped my men, and since I was unsure if you had worked out what I was up to, I decided to pay a little visit...to your mother.'

Ben felt like a pit had opened up beneath his feet.

'She was so pleased to see me, especially when I offered to take the twins off her hands for a trip to the zoo. Working at that gym of hers is so hard, isn't it? And your dad out all day and then all evening on the taxis...'

Ben saw red. How dare she? 'You...!' He wanted to smash that confident smile right off her face.

'Oh please, darling Benjamin. Violence won't solve anything. Think of your sisters. Nice and safe. Who knows what could happen to them...' She let the sentence tail off into the room like a wisp of smoke. 'In one way, you have the upper hand. I am at your mercy. But in another, I hold two very valuable cards. Perhaps we can do a deal?'

Ben felt sick. This woman was playing him and he had no choice. In the last twenty minutes, she'd gone from friend to foe to victim and back again. There was no need to even point the gun at her any more. Ben clicked the safety shut and slid it into his backpack.

'Believe me, they are safely hidden. And unlike a safe, I don't crack easily. Now go. Get out. I will ring you to arrange a little swap.'

'You mean, a trap!' Ben said. 'We'll come alright, but with the diamond hidden. You show us Grace and Mary and we'll give you the stone.'

'Of course, of course. You have every right to be wary. But don't think a twenty-pound bit of paste will fool my eyes. I'll ring you shortly. Let's hope your mother isn't growing too worried. She's snowed under with paperwork, am I right?'

Ben nodded miserably.

'Well, Aunty Reliza will happily have the twins overnight. Your parents will be almost pathetically grateful. I'm sure you don't want to be telling them or the police anything at all. Nod if you understand me!'

They nodded. Three puppets on a string. From

the frying pan into the fire. But what if you flee the flames only to find a volcano on your doorstep?

They turned round, leaving Ms Reliza collapsed in her chair and making the call. As they walked down the corridor, San noticed the woman's coat, hanging on a hook.

'Wait a mo!' he whispered. As the others broke their stride, San looked back towards the office to make sure he was out of sight. He checked the coat over. The breast pocket would be perfect. Women used bags. Of course it was empty.

As the huge front door swung shut behind them, Charlie turned to San.

'What was that about?'

'What's Ben's so-called family friend said. Back-up. You'll see.'

Ben wasn't even listening. His sisters! He could feel the tears welling up. They were pains, alright. But there was a difference between being annoying and being kidnapped.

San's phone vibrated. He picked up the text. At least Break was alright, but now they had a different problem altogether.

15. TACTICS

**Saturday 29 September, 7.50 pm –
that evening**

Ben's eyes followed the trails of red spots splattered across the floor. He couldn't believe it.

'Lance, do you know your ketchup bottle's sprung a leak?'

Lance looked round slowly. Given the state of the floor in his bedsit, it hardly made much difference. 'Sorry, I couldn't come up with anything more refined.'

The others sat on the floor or leaned against a sofa that had seen better days. No one was complaining as they tucked in.

'Beans on toast hits the spot for me!' said San.

Lance felt relieved. His single cooking ring

and decrepit toaster were hardly going to win Michelin stars.

Charlie finished up and winced as she passed her plate back to Lance.

'You ought to get that seen to.'

Charlie shook her head. 'I've fallen off galloping zebras at circus school and dislocated my shoulder on the flying trapeze. It's a graze.' After soaking up enough loo roll to block a toilet, the bleeding had finally stopped. The scar would be impressive.

'Fair enough.'

The miracle was that they were all in one piece. After meeting up at Lance's, Break had shared his tunnel experiences, making sure they all knew that the stunts he pulled should have made the record books. Once the food was finished, they chewed over the problem of the twins.

'The moment you lot are in there, she'll delegate to Dez to finish off the job. It'll be suicide by numbers.' Lance wasn't happy at all.

'That's where you come in!' said Break.

'Oh, please. Not another plan! My right hand is only now getting over the last one!' He showed them his swollen fingers to prove the point.

'You gotta help us!' said Ben. He was desperate, especially after going home to find his mother twittering on about how helpful her old school friend was. What could he say, when his silence had been bought? This was no adventure any more, not when family was involved. He paced up and down the tiny room, marvelling at how Lance could live in this cooped-up space.

'We need five costumes and five mannequins. Will that do it, San?' said Break.

San nodded. If he could get the wireless speakers up and running, they might be in with a chance.

Lance had a solution. 'You remember my fellow student, Enid?'

Break certainly did. The thought made him go all dreamy.

'Let me try her number.' He punched it out and waited. 'Enid. Hey. How are…really. That's great. Oh. Costume problem…and some mannequins. Can you…? Wonderful.' He put the phone down. 'Can't get a word in edgeways, but aside from that she's a brick. Time to put the kettle on!'

Aside from his purchase of fake diamonds, Lance had suddenly gone domestic. 'Found these at the pound shop. Bargain!' he said as he dunked teabags and poured milk into six brand new mugs, unsullied by grimy student friends. When they were all settled with their tea, the door flew open to reveal a girl whose name in no way suggested her looks.

She was tall, blonde and needed no make-up whatsoever. San, Ben and Break did the usual boy-reaction. They stared and then tried not to stare as Charlie gave a humph of disapproval.

'How lovely to see you all again. Hear you're having a clothes and modelling problem!'

'Yeah!' said Ben, jumping in. 'It's for our art show at school. Sort of comment on world terrorism...thingy.'

'Wonderful how they teach the youngsters these days, eh Lance?'

The three boys smarted at the word 'youngsters'.

'Tell me what you need and we'll see what these clothes-making fingers of mine can rustle up!' She spooned half a kilo of sugar into her mug and drained it in one swallow. 'Now write us a shopping list, and I'll do my best. A week, say?'

Ben's face fell. 'We need them by tomorrow afternoon, latest.' They'd already had a text from Reliza with a time but no place yet. She was playing careful. No wonder.

'Oh!' said Enid, her face registering puzzlement. 'But tomorrow's Sunday. Surely school is closed?'

There was a silence, which Lance tried to fill.

'What Ben means is that...'

'No!' said Ben. 'It's a good question and it deserves a fair answer.' Enid had helped them once before, with no idea of the true reason for her disguising Lance as an old Russian man. He decided to tell her this time. 'It's my sisters. They've been taken.'

Enid was finally stopped in her tracks. The tale that unfolded beat the plot of any stage production. 'Oh golly! Oh gosh!' she said, when Ben had finished. 'Is there any more tea?'

As Lance filled the kettle, Enid pulled out a pencil from behind her ear and began to rummage in her bag. She found a tiny notebook, opened it and began to write. 'We need to measure up my colleague first!'

Lance submitted to Enid measuring his vital statistics. 'You have to get out more, exercise, take up jogging!' she admonished as she noted down the figures.

Lance sighed. 'I'm not playing the part of a body-builder, you know!'

'Well. That should do! Off I go!' And she was as good as her word, snatching a final slurp of tea as she vanished out of the door, leaving only one word floating in the air: 'Tomorrow!'

'She's quite a girl,' said Lance.

'Yeah!' said Ben, San and Break in unison.

'Charlie, you need to rest that arm of yours. In fact, we could all do with a good night's sleep. Let's go home, watch TV, make small talk.' Break was running the show, but he was right. They were exhausted.

At 6 am the following morning, four sleepy teenagers were back at Lance's. D-day. Make or break.

'She won't ring yet,' said San stifling a yawn.

'I never knew this time of day existed!' complained Ben. Not that he'd slept much, tossing and turning. The few fevered dreams he remembered involved the twins on a merry-go-round, speeding up faster and faster as he tried to pull the lever. They loved every minute of it, riding the wooden horses up and down and shrieking with joy. But Ben could see that, any second, the wheel would come loose and the whole structure collapse into smithereens. A good old-fashioned nightmare. Waking was no better.

'Neither did I!' grunted Lance, turning over in his bed and trying to ignore the assembled gang.

San turned on his PDA. 'My gut instinct tells me that she'll have visited the meeting place already. This morning, she'll give Ben the runaround – by the time he's visited several phone boxes in response to her instructions, she'll assume that we won't have time to set her up or involve the police.' San grinned wickedly. 'But I like the old American saying my dad is so fond of – "*Assume* means making an *ass* out of *u* and *me*"!'

'Get on with it,' said Charlie. She'd checked on her mum and dad before slipping out. Both sound asleep.

'Give me a chance!' said San. 'One of the best gadgets my dad road-tested for *Gizmoid* magazine was a miniature TLR transmitter, about the size of a one-penny piece. The bit that counts is the dual conversion superheterodyne circuit with an 8 pole crystal filter...'

'I'm sorry for interrupting,' said Charlie. 'Actually, no I'm not. But do you use this kind of language to impress the girls?'

'No!' said San, mortally offended. 'If you'll let me explain. The tech stuff means that our little baby has a range of forty kilometres.'

Charlie was finally impressed. 'And that's what you slipped into Reliza's coat.'

'Not only that, but it just needed a very simple bit of coding to overlay her signal, received from my flash-card receiver with a GPS mapping program. When they did this in the old Bond movies it was science fiction. Now it's science fact. Look!' He put the PDA on the floor so that the screen revealed a tiny street map. In the middle, indicating the street they had visited the previous afternoon, a tiny dot pulsed.

'She's back from hospital then,' said Ben. 'How does that help us?'

'Oh, ye of little faith! I've been able to record the history of her movements on my internal memory card. Press rewind and watch her go!' San worked his button-pushing miracle and suddenly the flashing dot zipped through the streets of London like a turbo-charged full-stop. 'I've already eliminated the hospital and her extended visit to Baz's father, which only leaves one destination.' He paused to scroll the map to the right place. 'I can't guarantee it – but the address fits. Quiet part of town, non-residential. Funnily enough, when I refined my queries on the search engine, it came up with a recycled-cardboard factory.'

Ben remembered the fall from the roof and shuddered. Cardboard had saved them. Maybe they wouldn't be so lucky next time. 'Funny isn't the word.'

'Good work!' said Break. 'Let's sort out the details.'

An hour later, they heard huffing and puffing up the stairs. But no one tensed, even when a hand appeared round the door, followed by an arm and then a whole body. The head was bald, and the eyes not up to much. 'Morning!' came a cheerful voice from behind the mannequin. Enid was also tugging a bulging, impossibly purple bag.

Lance leapt out of bed and made a grab for his jeans, hoping against hope not to be spotted.

'I was right!' said Enid, noticing his spindly legs. 'Even my anorexic model here has more muscles than you!'

'I'm an actor!' said Lance, trying to do up his fly as he hopped about barefoot. 'It's my brain that's well-built!'

'I believe you,' said Enid, 'but there's no point hiding beneath those jeans. Time to try out my costume!'

Lance had had enough. He grabbed the bag from Enid's hand and stalked off to the bathroom.

'The rest of my silent friends are in the car,' continued Enid. 'Bit of a squeeze, but you let me know the delivery address. I spent all night working on them – it was one long dressing-up party!' She dropped the cheerful face for a second. 'Are you alright, Ben?'

'Yeah. No. The house felt...all wrong last night. Mum and Dad watched the box and she told him about all the capers she used to get up to with her school friend...'

'Don't worry, Ben. My men are professionals and the fact they aren't alive is no hindrance at all!'

Lance strode back in. Or rather, a very intimidating figure that bore some facial resemblance to Break's big brother. This person seemed older, larger, altogether more menacing. The heavy black boots and the peaked cap added to the ensemble.

'Oooh!' said Enid. 'I always like a man in uniform. I take back my earlier insults!'

'You'll do,' said Break. 'Time to go hunting!'

16. DOUBLE SETUP

Sunday 30 September, 7.23 am – five minutes later

Charlie felt sorry for Ben as they walked down the stairs. He was the one left with the phone, unable to do anything except play his part, which meant waiting until the call came. Meanwhile, they had work to do.

Outside the flats, their transport beckoned.

'I can't be seen in that!' said Break.

'But it's my family's pride and joy!' said Enid in a wounded voice as she stroked the side of the ancient camper van.

'It's brown!' protested Break, though a varying shade moving from beige through to rust and tinted mud would have been more accurate.

'Come on!' Enid slid open a protesting side

door and the others climbed in, apart from San, who had the privilege of sitting up front on the stained 70s velour-covered seats.

'Let's hope the police don't stop us!' laughed Charlie. A bunch of mannequins with fake weapons? This camping trip would take some explaining.

San checked his bag. The lapel-mic and speakers were in place, batteries recharged overnight. He fired up the digital assistant. After yesterday's events, he hoped Ms Reliza was still tucked up in bed. Even evil needed rest. He searched the frequencies, finally locking onto a signal. The pulsating dot reassured him.

'We're clear.'

Enid took that as a licence to stick her foot down on the accelerator. Nought to sixty in about five years. Once the camper was up to speed, she hared round corners as if her van weren't a rust-bucket but a Ferrari. The streets were quiet. The overnight rain had cleared, leaving the pavements looking as if they had been hand-polished.

As they pulled up outside the warehouse, Break noticed the slight chill in the air. Soon outdoor skating would vanish like the summer.

Charlie looked at the bulky padlock on the huge steel sliding doors and smiled. Why did people assume that bigger was better? A bent paper-clip and years of unofficial training from her retired father paid off. The padlock slid off its hasp. Her dad might not have approved, but it wasn't them committing the crime. She went to sit inside the van and play lookout while the mannequins were unloaded and shifted inside. After the gear had been moved, she put the padlock back on and clicked it shut. There was no going back now.

The others walked into what felt like a Tardis. Blank walls with high-up windows hid a space of aircraft-hangar proportions. A whole fleet of forklift trucks were lined up the side in Sunday silence. The objects of their lifting were compressed and stored on pallets along an enormous open gallery, with several floors running along both sides of the building. At either end, spiral ramps were installed for the vehicles to ascend and descend. It was recycling heaven. More importantly, it suited Break's purposes very well.

As Break directed, the immobile bodies were hauled into various positions between cardboard corridors, creating a perfect ring around the central open space on the concrete ground floor. Arms and legs were manoeuvred, fake weapons aimed.

San took a short break from studying the screen on his PDA, hoping that Reliza wouldn't decide to make an instant unannounced visit. They'd been here for over an hour now. Time was short. He ran up the spiral ramp with his bag of goodies, placing a speaker by each mannequin and inserting the batteries. He left Lance until last.

'Speak if you can hear me!' said San into the lapel-mic, now attached underneath the black padded jacket around Lance's shoulders.

'Course I can hear you!' protested Lance. 'Do I look like I'm made of fibreglass?'

His words appeared to come from five places at once, echoing round the building.

Enid looked up from her spot in the centre of the floor and gave the thumbs up. 'Loud and clear!' she said.

'Here's your remote,' said San to Lance. 'Very simple, sequential input. Press any number from one to five, and your voice will be projected from that speaker. Call it wireless ventriloquism!'

Lance settled down in the narrow gap. He felt like he was lying in a library of collapsed boxes, wondering which one to take home to read. The view was perfect.

Enid suddenly hissed.

San looked down as she made a frantic pointing motion with her arm back towards the door. At least the models were now hidden.

Enid ran for the shadows like an adrenalin-fuelled rabbit popping down a hole. The others took their cue. San now looked down on an empty, undisturbed area. He wondered whether a pigeon had startled her. His PDA reassured him. Reliza was not yet on the move.

Then he felt his phone vibrate and flipped it open to pick up the message. It was Charlie on lookout. San could have kicked himself. In trying to foresee all the moves, there was one he'd missed. The most obvious.

San was spot-on about phone games, thought Ben as he ended the call. Ms Reliza was up and about, no doubt looking for a wig for her bald head. But her voice had regained its poise and she was the one calling the shots. He had fifteen minutes to find the first phone box and wait for it to ring.

He took the stairs three at a time, glad to be on the move at last. Forget his board. This would take legs. He sprinted off down the road and round the corner. The early dog-walkers were out, doing their bit to add some colour to the streets – mainly brown. Ben ignored them, thinking about the game he loved playing with his sisters as he bounced them on his knee: *I want someone to buy me a pony, jig-jog-jig-jog-jigger-jog-jig...*

The phone was ringing as he screeched round the corner. An old lady with the Sunday papers looked as if she was going to answer it. Ben slipped in front of her and picked up the receiver.

'Hello again, Benjamin. Exercise is so good for you. I could tell you and your friends where to meet, but let's play this game for a little longer!' She directed him to another box, another street, as if he were a pawn in her game, shifting about the board further and further from safety.

An hour later he reached the fourth box, bending over to catch his breath. The phone kept on ringing. Let her wait. She finally told him where to go. It was on the next street, down an alley. He already knew, and hoped the others were ready as he loped round the corner, searching for a place to secrete an all too easily lost package.

After all this time, he was convinced that the stone in his mouth was acquiring a flavour. Sharp, bright, slightly sour. It beat chewing gum any day.

He was near now. His eyes scanned the street furniture. Where? There. A wall that had seen better days. Loose mortar. He used his front door key to gouge a hole about 10 centimetres above the pavement. As he pushed the stone in and used spit and the crumbled mortar to cover his hidey hole, he had a pang of grief. Goodbye little stone. For now. Time to meet and greet.

Dez stalked into the centre of the ground floor as if spotlit on a stage. But instead of pulling out a microphone, he withdrew a gun.

Lance tried not to breathe. It didn't help that the air was full of cardboard dust. His nose detected the foreign particles and began to quiver. Sneezed into oblivion – what a great end that would be. His fingers carefully squeezed his nose tight, telling it to behave. The nose decided to agree. Perhaps the body's immune system was not under attack after all. Lance breathed a silent sigh of relief.

Dez sniffed the air as if he were a hound on the scent. He turned full circle, his eyes taking in every detail, apart from the hidden ones, both living and fibreglass. He put the gun down on the ground and flipped open his phone. 'I'm in,' he growled. Call over. He picked up the gun and walked into the shadows, melting away as if he'd never been there in the first place.

Break crouched behind a bin. They should have gone for him when his gun was down. Too late. Of course Dez would be waiting for them. What he didn't know was that they'd got here first.

Now they all waited in the forced quietness, each of them trying to ignore cramp and itches. One movement, one inadvertent shuffle would give them away. The seconds passed slowly. Maybe nature was with them, as the wind picked up outside, rattling ancient window panes and stealing under the roof. The building filled with sounds, camouflaging them and giving hope. Maybe they wouldn't be noticed.

Five minutes went by. San had turned the sound off on his PDA. The bright spot was finally moving, slower, then suddenly faster. Walking, then driving. He scrolled the map, knowing exactly where the dot was heading. He switched off, mentally reviewing all the technicals in his head. What if the batteries failed? What if the wireless system packed up? But worry wasn't going to get them anywhere.

He heard a car draw up. Out of sight, a door opened, and the vibrating dot turned into a figure wearing a wig and dark glasses.

Charlie smiled. It would take more than a few trips to the beauty salon for the woman to get her hair back.

Ms Reliza's stilettos clicked on the concrete floor like gunshots. Even though her eyes were hidden, it felt like they were lasers seeing right through every hiding place.

'Ready?' she hissed.

'Yeah.' The voice that fell from the shadows seemed utterly confident.

It was showtime.

17. THE UPPER HAND

Sunday 30 September, 8.45 am – five minutes later

Ben made his entrance, playing it well. He tried to look uncertain, concerned but angry. Being cocky wouldn't cut it.

'Good morning, Benjamin. Nice of you to join us.' Ms Reliza made it sound like a tea party. 'But where are your friends?'

Ben wished Lance could do this bit. His skills were so much better. He swallowed. 'This is nothing to do with them. You were a friend of my mum's. It's for her sake. And the twins'. You have the stone. I get the twins. We walk away.'

For a second, there was a quiver in her features. Could she really have a conscience? He doubted it. As long as he could take her sharp mind off the others. 'Fine. Show me the stone.'

'Hidden,' said Ben. 'I want to see Mary and Grace first.'

'Have it your way!' Ms Reliza moved a hand towards her bag.

Break watched like a hawk. If she was intent on taking Ben out, maybe this was the moment to play. He had his finger on the send button, but something told him to wait.

Ms Reliza pulled out a phone, not a gun. 'The wonders of modern technology!' she sighed as she punched out the numbers and looked at the large screen. 'Hello, girls!' she said, 'Would you like to say hi to your brother?' She handed the phone over.

The picture was grainy and their movements jerked about. But Ben couldn't help smiling. It was them.

'Hallo Ven!' Mary lisped. Three years old and she still couldn't get his name right. He forgave her. Grace waved at him absent-mindedly as the portable DVD player she was watching held her attention. He could see they were in a van.

'Are you alright?' asked Ben, feeling shaky all over with a mix of relief and anger.

'We had choccy!' Mary squealed.

A hand cut across as the camera moved and

briefly rested on another face, leering out across the mobile network. 'See you later!' it smiled. Johnny. Still alive then.

Ben could make out a leg covered in plaster. The man deserved far worse than broken limbs.

'Satisfied?' said Ms Reliza, snapping the phone shut.

'What's to stop you taking me out once I give you the stone?' he demanded.

'Look in my bag! No gun. You took it, remember?'

Did she think he was stupid? All the better for him. 'I'll be back in a minute. Don't try to follow me.' Ben slipped out of the building.

As she smiled, Break felt sick. *Come on Ben. Let's do it.*

Ben returned a few minutes later, clenching his fist. 'Here!' he said through tight lips. His fingers unfurled and reached reluctantly towards Ms Reliza.

'Good for you!' she said, picking up the stone and bringing it to her eyes. She pulled at the loupe hanging round her neck to inspect the jewel carefully under the magnifying glass. The pink colour was pure and unsullied compared to the painted nails that held it. 'No fakery. None at all. This is my pension!'

'My sisters!' demanded Ben.

'Oooh! I don't think you are in any position to call the shots, little boy.'

Ben put on his best angry face. 'What game d'you think you're playing?'

'Endgame,' said Ms Reliza, as she snapped her fingers.

Dez walked out of the shadows on cue, his gun trained on Ben.

'Honour is a nice idea, Benjamin, the bonds of friendship and all that. But this is the modern world we are talking about. No hard feelings, eh? Dez will happily take care of your other friends when he's finished with you, isn't that right?'

'It'll be my pleasure!' said Dez. That little skateboarding git would be the first to feel his fury. It was nice to have things to look forward to in life. It was like popping a good spot. The moment it went *splat* was always the most satisfying. They'd escaped from him too many times. Enough was enough.

Ben put his hands up. His heart was pumping as he tried not to look around him.

Break didn't need to send his signal – Lance had years of going on stage at the right moment.

His voice came in right on cue. 'Hands up! Armed police marksmen! You're surrounded! Put down your weapon!' Each command came from a different direction as lights snapped on, revealing five rifles aimed directly at Dez and Ms Reliza. For an opening night show, they couldn't have asked for a better response.

Dez looked round, shock on his face. Outdone by a bunch of kids and now this. You don't mess with a trained marksman, not unless you fancy having your skull blown away. He dropped his gun. Ms Reliza dropped her smile.

It was over.

Charlie came through the open door, rope in hand, ready to tie Dez in knots. She savoured the droop of Ms Reliza's face and shoulders. The woman had nearly got away with it once. Not again.

'I suggest you ask your friend to bring my sisters in!' said Ben.

Lance stood up, speaking into a walkie-talkie that was in fact a painted mini cereal packet with an old straw stuck on the end. Who said props were useless? 'Back up, ready to enter the building now!' He only had to fool them for a few more seconds, until Charlie got going with her fingers and Ben picked up the gun. 'Step away from the weapon please, sir!' Lance's politeness was chilling.

Dez wavered for a moment, then did as he was told.

At that moment, there was a clattering sound. Several pairs of eyes swivelled round to see an object falling from one of the stacks to end up lying limply on the floor. Oh no! It was a hand. There was no bloody stump on the end of it, only a plug. As if to confirm its origin, one of the fingers broke off and rolled over the concrete like a pink, one-legged spider.

Dez's mind moved quickly and he burst out laughing. 'Fake marksmen!' He dived for his gun, rolling in one smooth motion, grabbing the weapon and landing on his feet before his startled audience. Charlie was in the way. He grabbed her and put the pistol to her head. Now she was the prop. 'You had some nerve! I'll give you that!' he said. 'But your little charade is over. Here,' he motioned to Ms Reliza. 'Let's start with tying this one up. I suggest the rest of you don't try anything spectacular, as bullets are faster than kids, any day!' He looked up at Lance. 'And put that toy rifle away, boy!'

Lance put it down. Enid was behind him, tears in her eyes. All because of one stupid little hand.

Break was still in the shadows, watching his perfectly planned plot literally fall apart. There was no back-up, no plan B, no police waiting round the corner. Unless he rang them. He could imagine the police operator on the other end of the line as he raved about stolen diamonds and kidnapping. The operator would laugh at first and then accuse him of wasting police time. Didn't he know they had real criminals to catch?

Break had suggested to Ben the night before that they bring Ms Reliza's gun. Ben had flared up.

'You are kidding! I don't fight fire with fire. We use guns, we're as bad as them!'

Break had given in at that point, and the gun was safely stashed under Lance's bed. Too late now.

'Come on!' said Dez. 'Let's have the rest of you then! Hide and seek won't do you any good now.'

The game was lost. San, Break, Enid and Lance stood up and made their way into the central floorspace, guided by Dez's gun.

Break did the numbers. Only one gun and six of them. Maybe if they rushed him? He'd only have time to fire off a couple of shots. Two down? He looked around at his friends. How could he lose any of them? He realised it wasn't worth it.

'Darling, darling Benjamin,' cooed Ms Reliza. 'I'm so sorry it turned out like this. Your plan was most ingenious, I have to *hand* it to you!'

Dez snickered at her joke.

'But now we have the upper hand, as it were!' She stamped on the fibreglass finger, crushing it like a useless insect. 'So here we are, far away from safety. I have the diamond. I also have all of you. I would ask you to introduce me to your other two accomplices...' she waved her arm in the general direction of Enid and Lance, 'but what's the point in getting to know them when our acquaintanceship is going to be cut short so soon?'

'You're insane!' said Ben. 'A stupid wig and a bit of make-up won't change that!'

'Thank you for reminding me about my... injuries. Let me assure you that Dez here will make sure you pay the full price. As for being mad?' She took off her dark glasses and fixed Ben with eyes beneath painted eyebrows instead of real ones. 'True. I am mad about beautiful objects. This one in particular will help keep me in the lifestyle to which I am accustomed. Goodbye, all of you. And Benjamin, at least I will let you speak one last time to your sisters. All yours, Dez!' She turned away as if the whole bunch of them were nothing more than dust and bent over to retrieve her bag.

18. SERIOUS MOVES

Sunday 30 September, 9.03 am – one second later

The comment about his sisters was all he needed. Anger rose up in him, fierce and sharp. Everything had to be used to his advantage, even insults. Ben's mind worked overtime. He could see Ms Reliza bending over, hear the command issuing from her lips, watch as Dez's brain took in the information. She spoke, he listened.

And although he was a professional, although this was his day job, even Dez couldn't help the slight movement of his eyes. After all, the boss was speaking. She was his employer and there was big money in this job, if he finally got it right. No more mortgage. He could open up a proper bike shop, rather than working out of some grotty garage under the railway arches. There would be others to do the grease-monkey work and he could sit in an office and bark out orders. Maybe he could even go straight? Big bikes cost money and the margins were decent enough.

Ben could see all this: the momentary daydream in Dez's eyes, the one millisecond where his finger was not totally focused on the trigger, the mistake of letting his attention waver as he paid homage to Ms Reliza. At the same moment, Ben's own thoughts were working out odds and distances – instant calculations firing off the synapses in his brain.

This was the true art of free-running. The urban landscape was nothing more that a set of immovable obstacles, strung out like pearls with the athlete threading their way between them. As each foot fell, as each breath roared into the lungs, eyes and brain already moved onto the next block, the next jump, the next set of stairs.

So, think of Dez as another obstacle. How to tackle him? Imagine he's a wall. It was that simple.

All this in a blink of an eye. Ben's breathing had already slowed and his right foot led off with perfect instinct. Use Dez's confidence against him. Who would attack a man with a gun? Ben said that Ms Reliza was insane. So was he. The body moving forwards now, uncoiling, left foot down to act as the spring. He bent his knee to crouch and took off.

Dez clocked him, saw the sudden set of movements out of his left eye. He began to swivel, years of surviving the street gangs helping his arm to come up.

Ben was flying now, feet first. An angry missile of flesh, blood and bone. If he was to bounce off the wall, what he needed above all was impact, the perfect aim to hit the honey spot. Ben's anger was true and honest. He straightened his legs right at the moment his feet connected with Dez's chest. Two cracks, one shot and Dez was down, the gun flying through the air. Ben felt a far off punch in his shoulder. His brain told him it was nothing. Ignore it for now. Two cracked ribs, a good sign. And the wall that was Dez was crumbling, toppling over, smashing to the ground, out cold.

This was only half the move though. Ben continued, using Dez's bulk as a gift, a diving board. As Dez fell, Ben crouched and bounced off his chest, back into the air, as if land was a mere stopping-off point on an endless aerial journey. Ben was no longer out to impress anyone, didn't care if they talked about it later, wasn't bothered about applause.

He rolled through the air backwards, somersaulting away at an angle.

Ms Reliza scrabbled in her bag, knew that it was almost too late as she pulled out a shiny object, clicked it to reveal the blade. Flick-knife. Most unladylike.

As Ben flew, all old bonds of friendship were ripped away by his streamlined body. He couldn't possibly see the knife, but he didn't care. He was in the zone now. That's all there was. And for the second time, his feet did the work for him. What good was a tiny metal edge against sixty kilos of airborne muscle?

Before she could even begin to stab, Ms Reliza was shoved backwards by the force of his landing. The cracking sound was the most satisfying of all, as her arm suddenly flopped at an angle nature never intended. The useless knife skittered away over the floor. One move, two down.

Mouths dropped open as Ben stood, bent over, sucking the breath into his lungs as if he'd almost drowned.

Dez was out cold, and Ms Reliza whimpered as she tried to retreat across the floor like a wounded crab.

Break grabbed Dez's gun. It was over. For real. 'Are you alright, Ben?'

Ben looked up, dazed. 'Don't know. Feel weak. I...'

As his eyes began to glaze over, Charlie ran to his side to catch him before he fell. Blood seeped out over his T-shirt. She laid him down gently on the ground, using her jacket as a pillow. 'You've been hit.'

'Good guess!' he grimaced as the adrenalin began to wear off. Charlie ran for Ms Reliza's knife and begin to slice away his T-shirt. The blood was pouring out of his shoulder now.

'We need an ambulance!' she shouted.

San flipped open his phone and made the call as Charlie tried to stanch the flow of blood.

'You saved us, Ben. You did it!' And suddenly they were all clustered round him, amazed at what he'd pulled off and frightened of the consequences.

'Yeah!' Ben's eyes opened in sudden panic. 'Mary and Grace?' he began to flail about, trying to stand up. He had to get to his sisters, injury or no injury.

'Leave it to me!' said Break, sprinting towards the main door. He hoped that Johnny hadn't heard the gunshot.

Lance ran after him. 'You need me?'

'Yeah. Good one!' he said as they ran, explaining what Lance had to do.

It made sense that the van was parked nearby. Break hoped that Johnny had taken precautions. As they rounded the corner, his guesswork proved right. Behind the tinted windows, he could make out curtains, drawn tight to protect the vehicle from prying eyes. Johnny's problem was that, while no one could see in, he couldn't see out.

Lance ran at a crouch towards the sliding door. He turned to his brother, who gave him the thumbs up.

Lance lifted his hand and slammed it against the door. 'Let me in, you moron!' The voice was perfect, an angry imitation of Dez. If Break shut his eyes, he could almost see the tattooed tear.

'Yeah, yeah! Wait a mo,' came the muffled voice from the other side. The door slid open. As it did, Lance reached in, grabbed an arm and pulled hard. By this time, Break was in position, right beside his brother.

Johnny flew out, the words 'Where's Dez?' fading fast from his lips.

Lance stepped out of the way, leaving Break to place himself in the way of Johnny's fall.

And Johnny was no expert skater. One bad fall deserved another. His exit from the van was short, sharp and to the point. He landed hard on the pavement, his one good leg bent back awkwardly.

'Oh dear!' said Break. 'One broken leg is bad luck. But two? That's merely stupid!'

Johnny howled in agony and the sound was finally loud enough to distract the twins from their DVD.

Mary and Grace were sat on the car seats surrounded by empty sweet wrappers. They looked puzzled for a second, but when they saw Break, smiles broke out over their dimpled faces.

'Come on, girls. Time to take you home! Are you hungry?'

While Lance stood guard over the incapacitated Johnny, the girls nodded enthusiastically as Break took them each by the hand and led them to freedom.

19. JUST DESERTS

Saturday 13 October, 2.35 pm –
two weeks later

The Olatunjis' living room had never been so full and Mrs O was running out of mugs for tea.

Ben had pride of place, propped up on the sofa, his shoulder swathed in bandages, as the rest of the gang tried to stuff him full of biscuits.

'If I'd known what you were up to, boy!' His mother gave him a look of both fury and tenderness.

'Exactly. You would have stopped us. But I'm sorry, yeah. Really.' He looked over at the twins, playing dressing-up games with costume tiaras and plastic diamond necklaces. Why did he get involved in the first place?

'You're here now. That's what counts. What that

so-called friend of mine did was unforgivable! To waltz in here after all these years and almost destroy our family… I believed her. She seemed so concerned about how tired out we were. I let her take the twins away!' Her lips began to quiver.

Ben's dad looked ashamed. 'My fault too,' he muttered.

'She fooled all of us,' Break said.

'She did. Always up to something, that one.' Mrs Olatunji looked distant for a second, remembering. 'More detentions than I could count! We all looked up to her at school. And the way she dealt with that boy who was givin' me hassle!' She shook her head. 'She sure changed a lot. When I came down to pick up the rest of you at the police station and caught a glimpse of her in the cells, I hardly recognised her.'

'That was thanks to me!' Charlie said brightly. She had no regrets on that score. Sometimes you *could* fight fire with fire.

'She wouldn't even look at me! I hope they send her down for a very, very long time.'

When San had rung 999, it had taken all his persuasive powers to convince the woman on the end of the line that it was no hoax. The paramedics arrived first and got straight down to business. Apart from working to stop Ben bleeding, this meant mainly reassuring the others that it looked like a flesh wound. Plenty of red stuff, but dying was not on the cards – though Ben kept insisting he was.

As Ben was carted off in the ambulance, the police scratched their heads at Johnny, Dez and Ms Reliza, all trussed up like turkeys and moaning in pain in the middle of a recycling warehouse. Normally, the police were called because their expert help was needed. But the only job they could do was mopping up and suffering the endless screeched excuses of some woman trying to stop her wig falling off. According to her, this bunch of evil teenagers were about to murder the lot of them.

Only when Ben reached into her handbag, pulled out the perfect piece of sparkling pink stone and reluctantly handed it over to the officer in charge did Ms Reliza finally fall silent. The arrests were made and days of interviews began, with the police increasingly incredulous about what Ben and the others had achieved. But who cared what they thought, anyway?

Break grabbed baby Thomas out of his rocker and threw him up in the air. Thomas gurgled with delight. If he could have said the word 'more', he would have done. Flying was fun. 'Your boy will make a fine skater one day!'

'Oh, no!' Mrs Olatunji shook her head. 'One injured child is enough, no thanks to you lot!' She glared at Ben. 'Maybe I should ban your friends from ever coming round again?' She looked at San, Charlie, Break, Lance and Enid. No one met her gaze. 'Still, that would mean they couldn't sample my excellent curry. And where would we be then?' The tension faded and smiles broke out across the assembled company.

'Mrs O?' San had a puzzled look on his face.

'Yes?'

'When we found Ms Reliza's office, the nameplate didn't make sense.'

Everyone looked at San as if he were going bonkers.

'What do you mean?'

'It said Ms R. Eliza not Ms Reliza.'

'Oh that,' said Mrs Olatunji, with a smirk on her face. 'We ought to feel sorry for her, really.'

'Never!' hissed Ben.

His mother continued. 'Her father wanted a boy and out popped a girl instead. He couldn't bear it. Called her Rudolf!'

'You're joking!' said Break.

'No. She told the story once. Her mother had

a fit and threatened divorce, but at the last minute managed to have it changed to Rudolfa! At school she tried to keep it secret, but every time she came into class there was a chorus of a certain well-known song involving reindeer!'

Everyone burst out laughing.

'No wonder she turned out evil!' Charlie said. 'Her name's already a crime!'

'With that mystery solved, it's time for me to attend to the food. Husband of mine, some help would be appreciated!' As Mrs O vanished into the kitchen, followed by her obedient other half, the doorbell rang.

'Oh no, not more visitors!' groaned Ben.

Charlie opened the door and they could all hear murmurs in the hall. Two men came in. One was old, wearing wrinkles as if they were the latest fashion. The other was in uniform.

PC Smythe scowled. It was what he did best. Without any hellos, he launched off. 'Plenty of charges I could have you under – breaking and entering, grand theft, withholding information, disturbing the peace – let alone the traffic bylaws you lot always choose to ignore...'

He was interrupted by Ben's mother. 'PC Smythe. How nice to see you. Would you like a cup of tea?'

The man was flustered, thrown off-balance for a second. 'Well, I...'

'Let me guess. Are you a milky, two sugars man?' She smiled sweetly.

'Yes. How did you... But as for your offspring and his accomplices...'

'Were you ever a teenager?' Ben's father asked him. He'd been quiet so far, but this officer was standing in his living room. 'You see, I was once. And I have a vague memory of that time.' He winked at his son.

Ben was impressed. It was nice to have his dad stick up for him for a change.

'It's an irrelevant question. I...'

Mr Tirov had had enough. Age was no barrier to being assertive. 'PC Smythe. We agreed when we came along today that this would be a discussion, not a catalogue of threats!' His voice had authority.

Everyone fell silent.

'You could call this motley selection of teenagers a bunch of thieving layabouts. Or not.' He paused and let his ancient but sharp eyes fall on each one of them.

'They acted out of a sense of honour. A rare word these days, I grant you, but one that is invaluable. As far as they saw it, an old family friend had been duped. I was painted as a great rogue. I also have a feeling that when this young gentleman here,' he pointed at Ben, 'dropped a certain stone of mine on the floor during their school visit, my temper was not what it should have been. I spoke harshly to my secretary and snapped at him. For them it merely confirmed the story they had been told.'

Ben nodded. It was as if Ms Reliza had set up his own clumsiness. It meant they had fitted Mr Tirov's actions into her web of lies.

'Their only aim was justice, and the way they went about it? Ingenious! Jumping between buildings, climbing through roofs, beating my alarm system and then, to top it all, the matter of the safe.' Tirov was on a roll now, his eyes glinting brighter than any stone. 'You have done the security companies a big favour by revealing their weaknesses. I would not be surprised if further work comes your way.'

PC Smythe wasn't going to give up so easily. 'All that as may be, but they still broke the law!' he whined.

'Oh, give it up, man. I'm not going to press charges. The stone has been recovered and is soon up for auction. When Ms Reliza and her two real accomplices have got over their injuries, they will no doubt be taking up residence at Her Majesty's pleasure. If anything, young Benjamin and his friends should receive awards for their bravery.'

Ben's dad smiled. This was more like it.

At this point, Mrs O pushed a hot mug into PC Smythe's hand. It was the signal for defeat. He sipped his tea sulkily as Tirov went round the room shaking each of his former and imagined enemies by the hand.

'To see such skill has made me feel young again. Thank you so much!'

Mr Tirov said his goodbyes and literally pulled the policeman out of the room behind him.

'Now what?' said Charlie.

Break looked out of the window. Clear and crisp, early Autumn in the air, leaves going brown. The city and all its surfaces were dry. 'I have an idea!' he said. 'But first, I smell something very tasty.'

As if his nose were a magic wand, plates of food appeared out of the kitchen, piled high with steaming hot rice, curry filled with fresh coriander, ginger, garlic and endless spices, served alongside little pots of yoghurt with diced cucumber and home-made mango chutney.

'You're the best, Mum!' said Ben, raising his glass.

'And can we have some praise for the skivvy who chopped the onions, ground the spices and generally acted as a slave to Her Kitchen Highness?' Ben's dad pouted.

'To Mr and Mrs O!' everyone cheered in unison. It was time to tuck in.

Forty-five minutes and a bus ride later, the kids stood outside their familiar place.

'What's the point of me coming out with you?' Ben complained. His shoulder still throbbed under the bandages. The doctor said it would be a few weeks yet before he could start on physio. It was going to be a long break from free-running.

'Fresh air's good for you,' answered Break. 'And we can make sure you see how much fun you're missing out on!'

'Thanks a lot! Instead of bowing down and worshipping me as your saviour. I'm insulted.'

'Fair enough!' said Charlie and gave him a curtsy. The others bent over and flourished their arms as if he were indeed a king. Ben acknowledged his loyal subjects.

'My good people. I now release you from your duties as crime-fighters extraordinaire. Go forth and skate!' As Ben walked behind, the rest of them zipped and flipped their way through the street section of the park, heading towards the holy grail of skatedom – the bowl.

They looked round at their fellow skaters. Would they believe a word of what they told them or think it was all a fevered fantasy? It didn't matter. Today there were no chases, no dressed-up *femmes fatales*, no dangerous confrontations apart from those between board and bowl.

Break dropped and rode, pumping for speed, hitting rails and sending up sparks, pulling outrageous air to the slap and clap of decks. He was home at last.

Charlie played differently. To her, it wasn't about pulling slick tricks, but more about flow and grace as she snaked round the curves and slid along the vert.

Even San was up for it. Maybe today he would drop in for the first time ever. The experienced skaters gave him room as he began to balance his tail on the edge. But before he could take the rollercoaster risk, he felt a shove from behind.

'Why are you always in my way, Car-Crash Kid?' sneered a familiar voice.

San swayed, and almost fell into the bowl. He managed to regain his balance before turning round. The others were at the far end of the park, tucking into their crisps and cokes. He was alone. In front of him stood the last person he wanted to see. Fuzz for hair, a bulky blob on a bike.

'You lot!' Baz hissed. 'My uncle's got two broken legs and my dad's ribs are shattered. Thanks to you, they're off to prison!' He leered closer, his fists bunching up ready for take off. 'And it's up to me to look after the family honour!'

San was normally the first one to stutter, shrink away, do anything to flee the danger. He surprised himself. 'What do you know about honour? And don't call me that anymore!'

'Or you'll what? Cry and go off to mummy? Oh, I forgot, you don't have one!' Baz's mates, slouching around on their oversized toddler bikes, laughed out loud.

By now, the whole park had fallen silent. No one was snaking in to ride the bowl. This was where the action was.

Out of the corner of his eye, San could see Charlie, Break and Ben slowly sidling towards him. They wouldn't make it in time. He was sick of having to be protected, sick of hiding behind his computer screen.

'You know, that mouth of yours really needs rearranging!' San stared at Baz, a wild look in his eyes.

'Ooooh!' went the others.

Baz laughed. 'I think you'll find it's the other way round, mate!' His fist shot forwards, ready to smash San's new-found confidence and pound it into the ground.

San saw it coming. It was time to see if all those Thursday nights had paid off.

His teacher was always going on about the predictability of attack. A punch in the face was obvious. And if it was obvious, it could be countered. San wasn't interested in the names of the moves, only their effectiveness. He ducked and Baz's fist whistled through empty air.

Before Baz had a chance to even question why San was no longer in the firing line, he felt a stab of pain.

It was all about being fluid. Flowing one movement into the next. Like skating, really. Ducking down required San to crouch, bend his knees, bring himself lower than his enemy. This was ultimately to his advantage, as it gave the momentum for his right knee to shoot up again and forwards right into the area most boys like to be avoided. San had no desire to go in softly, softly. His teacher had talked about the wind and now San understood. The wind was never half-hearted. If it was going to knock over a tree or lift a roof, then it had to be one hundred per cent. Force needed momentum and momentum required total conviction.

San's knee connected like a hammer. The high-pitched squeal from Baz confirmed that the target had been attained.

As Baz doubled over, clutching between his legs, it was San's turn to curl up his fingers in a tight ball and defend his family's honour. *This is for you, Mum,* he said to himself as his fist smashed into Baz's nose. A sickening crunch was followed by a river of red.

It was Ben's turn to look shocked. 'Way to go, San! Where'd you learn to do that?'

'Oh, here and there. Not only a geek, you know!' His fist hurt, but the pain was a good feeling.

'Ah! Your busy Thursday nights!' said Break, 'The mystery has finally been solved!'

San gave a little bow. The hard work, the endless sweaty practice had finally produced a result.

By this point, Baz lay spluttering on the ground, staining the concrete and moaning quite convincingly. The other bikers suddenly noticed they were outnumbered five to one by skaters. The odds didn't look good. Abandoning the leader made much better sense than hanging around. They turned their handlebars and cycled off.

Baz tried to stand up as he held his nose. 'I'll...I'll...'

'You'll what?' said Break. 'Bleed a lot? Go home and grow up, Baz. Your mum must be sick of looking after delinquents.'

San couldn't help himself. As Baz crawled towards his bike, San knelt over and whispered in his ear. 'You mention any member of my family again and this is the least I'll do!' San stood up and ran towards Baz's bike. Leaping up into the air, Baz cried out.

'Nooooo!'

The word had no effect. Total conviction. San came down feet first with a crash into the back wheel. Spokes bent and very expensive rims warped. 'Oh dear! Accidents happen, you know!'

Baz looked at his bike and burst out crying as he dragged the mangled wreck away.

'That was vicious!' said Ben.

'But very enjoyable. And you can hardly call your bone-cracking move an act of mercy!' San was on a roll. He'd dealt with one problem and dismissed Baz entirely from his mind. No point stopping now. He grabbed his board and balanced it on the lip of the shallow end of the bowl.

'Remember. All you have to do is commit to it. Don't hold back!' advised Break.

Break's words drifted like diamond dust through his mind. San looked down and realised that all he needed was gravity. It was now or never. Cliff jumping looked easy compared to this one-metre drop. He pushed hard with his front foot on the nose of the board and let his body follow through.

One second later, and he was still alive, still connected to his deck as he wobbled up the other side. It might not have been Tony Hawk, but it would do for him. Oh yes! The skaters went wild, their boards slamming harder and harder onto the edges, their applause ringing out through the park, across the city and rippling into the cold autumn sunshine.